BRITISH BACHELOR

USA TODAY BESTSELLING AUTHOR

K.K. ALLEN

Copyright © 2021 by K.K. Allen and Cocky Hero Club, Inc.

Editing and Proofreading: Red Adept Editing
Cover Design: BookCoverKingdom
(www.bookcoverkingdom.com)
Photographer: CJC Photography

Contact SayHello@KK-Allen.com with questions

ISBN: 9798598320051

BRITISH BACHELOR

USA *TODAY* BESTSELLING AUTHOR

K.K. ALLEN

To anyone who shares my love with the Bachelor franchise.
Yes, I took my obsession to the next level,
and I had so much fun doing it!

Dear Chelsea,

I know what you must think of me now that my secret is out, and I can't say I'm not disappointed. I bloody loved that you saw me as someone other than the bloke my entire country has deemed unworthy of love. Maybe I am, but that doesn't stop me from wanting you as desperately as I do.

Before you toss this letter in the rubbish bin, just hear me out.

Soon, I'll need to return home to face the critics—the harsh reminder of the man they all believe me to be, the *Forever Bachelor*—and you'll continue to live out your dreams here while nannying the twins. Simon and Bridget are so very lucky to have you.

All I ask is for one night with you, one night to remove the facade we've exhibited for the past two weeks to mask our true feelings.

Because I want you, Chelsea Banks, more than I've wanted

any woman in my entire life, and I dare to imagine that you might just want me too.

Even if just for one night.

Liam

1

CHELSEA

The bell above the door chimed as I pushed my way into the quaint Victorian building in Wayland Square, a historic area on the east side of Providence, Rhode Island. One look at the corner establishment with a hanging sign that read Spill the Tea could easily trick a person into thinking it was owned by an actual Brit. The truth was, my parents had just traveled to Europe one too many times.

The locals didn't mind who ran their favorite gossip joint. They came for the social hour, gathering at round tables while the mounted televisions around the room played delayed British news and drama shows. Guests loved their afternoon tea and the array of fancy finger foods offered, and my parents loved the guests right back.

"Oh, it's Chelsea," greeted a bubbly brunette named Gwen. She sat at a round table by the window with a few other women, all frequent visitors to the small tearoom and all around my mother's age. They loved to adopt English accents while they chatted, and with seemingly nothing better to do, they were also oddly curious about my personal life.

Groaning internally, I forced a friendly smile while slowing my walk toward the front counter. Since my mom was helping a customer, it would be obvious if I avoided the woman like I wanted to.

"Hi, Gwen. How's the tea today?"

She raised her cup, pinky out, and nodded her approval. "Absolutely delicious." She looked past me to the door that had just closed behind me. "Where are those little rascals who usually accompany you?"

Gwen was referencing the three kids I nannied for full-time—three-year-old twin girls and a twelve-year-old boy. Their parents worked at the hospital, Simon as a doctor and Bridget as a nurse. Two months ago they'd hired me to live in their pool house and watch the kids while they worked. Conveniently, their house was within walking distance from Spill the Tea, so we often strolled around the nearby park before stopping in for treats on our way back home.

When I didn't answer her quickly enough, Gwen's face fell into exaggerated sympathy. "Oh no. You are still employed, aren't you, dear?"

I let out an awkward laugh. "Yup. Still employed. They're just on a family holiday in Europe visiting their grandparents." I decided to leave my response vague. I always felt like the woman was fishing for something to elaborate on.

"Oh, that sounds splendid." Gwen set her tea down and placed her hands in her lap. "I do hope you're making the most of your days off." She eyed my hot-pink leggings and fitted black tank top with a frown. "I'm sure, with a bit of sprucing up, a pretty girl like you could easily attract a nice young lad around town. Maybe work on getting a few rascals of your own soon."

I groaned inwardly, regretting my decision to allow the conversation as I walked in. There was no hope of this going anywhere good. Gwen was as old-fashioned as they came, and I was certain that, in her eyes, being single in my late twenties was some sort of sin. Not that she was the only one in the joint who would have loved to see me hitched by then. I threw a sharp accusing glance at my mother, who was still helping a guest from behind the counter.

My mother had been talking about her future grandbabies since the day I'd graduated high school. It was like she'd had it all mapped out for me. I would go to college, meet a man, graduate, get married, then have a litter of babies. Nearly twelve years later, and my life hadn't panned out that way at all. I just wished my mother wouldn't be so open with her customers about my situation.

"For sure." I broadened my smile at Gwen to appease her after her rascal comment.

"Well, good. I'd hate to see a pretty girl like you wind up alone."

I'd had my share of boyfriends over the years, but after my most recent breakup, I knew the last thing I needed was another man in my life. It was time to focus on me, on dreams, my journey, my happiness. I felt stronger than I had in years, and I wanted to enjoy that time until the right man came along. Unfortunately, my mom and her old-fashioned friends would never understand. A woman like Gwen wouldn't want to hear that. She only wanted the juicy gossip, even if it was as fake as the jewelry she wore.

It took all my energy to keep the smile on my face. "Oh, I'm not alone. I just stopped by to get my tea and scone fix before the big night."

Gwen's eyes brightened, and she clapped her hands excitedly. "The big night, eh? Oh, do tell. Do you have a date? Is he as handsome as Dean?"

I cringed at the mention of my ex-boyfriend. I dropped him right along with college. He hadn't understood my need to pursue my dreams of writing, and that was enough for me to let him go. "Well, actually—"

Gwen cut me off, leaning forward as if no one else in the joint could hear her prodding questions and asking, "Is he the one?"

"Well, I don't know—"

"C'mon, dear," she jumped in again. "What does your gut tell you?"

With every interruption, my frustration grew. Still, I maintained my calm. "It's all too new to—"

"Have you shagged him yet?"

I heard my mom's gasp clear across the room. "Gwen!" she scolded. "Hush and leave the poor girl be. Who Chelsea chooses to *shag* is none of your business."

Holy hell. My eyes darted around the tearoom to see every single eyeball staring back at me except for the man at the counter who was thumbing through a stack of cash. But just because he wasn't gawking at me didn't mean he hadn't heard the entire exchange. Heat flooded my face as I rolled my eyes up to the ceiling, wishing I could crawl beneath the baseboards.

"As a matter of fact." Anger bubbled inside me as I faced Gwen with a syrupy smile. "We shag *all* the time. Morning, noon, and night. He's got a giant willy too. Huge." I held my hands apart and watched my audience's eyes bulge from their heads.

For the first time since I'd met Gwen, her poise faltered as she turned a shade that resembled the eggplant she was probably imagining. "That's good, dear." Gwen smiled weakly.

I bit back a laugh. "It was nice seeing you ladies again. It's always a pleasure." I curtsied, hoping Gwen could read through the gesture to see the "fuck you" clearly written beneath my niceties. Then I turned toward the front counter of the tearoom, where my mom was staring at me with her mouth hanging open.

The customer she'd been helping mumbled his quiet thanks, grabbed his hot tea from the counter, and turned toward the exit—toward me. One look at him and my steps slowed once more.

Dark shades covered his eyes like he'd stepped out of a limo onto a red carpet. He wore a black-and-gray zip-up hoodie over a plain white T-shirt and faded black jeans with large tears at the knees. Ink covered both his arms, which were visible below his pushed-up sleeves.

The man had a presence that made the entire room fade away, forcing my gaze to lock on him. And damn, I was transfixed.

He was heartrendingly gorgeous with just enough scruffy beard covering the lower half of his face that I could still see the sharp angles of his jaw, which sent blood pumping furiously through my veins. His wavy light-brown hair was tossed around his head like he'd forgotten to shower. It was like he knew he didn't even need to try.

We were a few steps from crossing paths—so close I could breathe in his cool, crisp scent—when he looked at me. At least it felt like he looked at me. His shades were too dark to tell for sure, but the way the corner of his mouth tipped up with just a hint of a smile rattled my insides to my core.

It was unfair. He could see me, but I couldn't see him. My disappointment was short-lived since, in the next second, he was out of sight—nearly out of mind. If it weren't for the husky words that slipped from his throat after crossing my path, I would have already been on my way toward forgetting about him completely.

"That's one lucky willy," he said in a deep voice from behind me. "Happy shagging, love."

His arrogance swirled through the air, thickening quickly and steadily, while embarrassment flooded my body and goose bumps rose beneath my skin. I dared a look over my shoulder to watch the strange man exit the tearoom. He carried a nonchalance in his walk. His tone was unmistakably British—the real accent, not the fake one Gwen and her friends liked to attempt.

I made a sound in the back of my throat to demonstrate the disgust I felt for the exchange I'd just had with Gwen. Then I turned toward my mom, who was eyeing me with a warning.

"Big plans tonight, huh?"

I let out a heavy sigh and shook my head while setting my elbows on the counter. "No, Mom." I kept my voice quiet enough so only she could hear. "I just wanted to get Gwen off my back. I stopped by to pick up tea and scones so I can go back to the Hogues' place—*alone*. I'm looking forward to a quiet night. No shagging, I promise."

Her lips twitched with a threatening smile, then she turned to grab my things she'd already prepared. "Well, in that case, enjoy it. But—"

I cringed at the conversation I knew was about to follow. *Here we go again.*

"Getting back out there isn't an entirely bad idea, sweetheart. You've been single for quite a while."

With a pinch of my lips, I pushed my exasperation back down into my chest, where I would continue to let it brew. "Two months." My words were quiet, measured. "That's hardly a long time."

"But you were with Dean for two years. The clock's ticking." She tapped her wrist as if that would drive her point home.

I reached over the counter and snatched the bag of scones and hot tea waiting for me. "You should be happy I got out of that relationship before it was too late."

She tilted her head with a squint. "You never did tell me what happened between you two."

Discomfort swarmed in the pit of my stomach. The fact that I'd dropped out of law school before fall semester classes had even started wasn't something I'd told my parents yet. They suspected my heart had never been in my studies since I had been perfectly content staying on the slow track—acquiring credits while I worked full-time—but they maintained the belief that my life wouldn't start until I had my business degree in hand. They were almost as bad as Dean when it came to my dreams of writing for a living.

"We were wrong for each other, plain and simple. I'm happy. Please be happy for me."

"Of course, I'm always happy if you are. I'm just not convinced that's the case. You're almost thirty, Chelsea. I thought I'd have grandbabies by now."

"Are you serious? I still have plenty of time."

"But—"

"*Please.*" I emphasized the word with a laugh. "Stop it. You'll get your grandbabies one day. I just need to find the right willy first." I winked and turned from the counter, ready to flee and never return. I was so relieved to see that Gwen and her friends had left.

Once I made it to the door, I looked back with a final wave. "Oh, and tell Daddy I stopped by. Just—try to leave out the willy talk."

With that, I stepped onto the sidewalk and headed in the direction of the Hogues' home. Alone.

2

CHELSEA

I took the long way back to Doctor Simon and Bridget Hogue's home on Blackstone Boulevard, sipping my tea and strolling by the park to watch the sunset before finally entering their private subdivision, lined by well-lit streetlamps that stood out against the darkening sky. I approached the half-acre property where an English-style brick manor home sat and veered right toward the wrought iron gate that led to the back of the house.

I punched the security code into the keypad and closed it behind me then followed the path toward the brightly lit private pool in the rear courtyard. For the past two months, I'd made a home of the small pool house, which was equipped like a small apartment with a bedroom, a bathroom, a small kitchen, and a living area. Most of my time was spent in the Hogues' main home with the kids, but during my off-hours, I was grateful for the small space I could call my own.

After closing the door behind me, I quickly traded my yoga attire for a tank top and cotton shorts, then strolled to my vintage record player—my pride and joy—and started up my new vinyl record by The 1975 that had been on repeat since it had come in the mail. Once the music was set, I tore into my takeout bag and pulled out the fresh scones, faux clotted cream, and jam. I was in pure heaven.

Entire days off at the Hogues' manor was scarce. They were more than decent employers, always ensuring I took time off, but with their jobs at the hospital, it was rare for them to have a full day—let alone week—off together, which meant I was always starting or ending my shift at irregular hours. I planned to relish my week without responsibilities, with nothing but my muse churning inspiration in my mind.

When my belly was completely satisfied, I reached for my blue notebook and lay stomach-down on the couch. I took up my black pen that bookmarked the page I had last scribbled some thoughts on and settled for a moment, rereading what I'd written that morning. They were largely character-development notes about a book I'd already written six drafts of but couldn't drum up the courage to let out of my clutches. I just kept picking it apart, chapter by chapter, until the story had evolved in ways I'd never imagined.

After making the decision to drop out of grad school to nanny full-time and write more often, not a single day had gone by in the past two months that I didn't wonder if I'd made a horrible decision. I was giving up the safety of a great education and potentially a large-salaried job for what? An unexplored writing career? It felt crazy to think about, but I didn't want to spend my time regretting not following my dreams. I wanted to spend my time *bringing them to life*.

I'd only started to make some additional book notes when I grew heavy with exhaustion. My pen fell from my hand, and my eyes drifted closed. Darkness settled over me while The 1975 lulled me into deep relaxation. The calm didn't last long.

My entire body startled awake at the sound of rock music

blaring right outside my door. *What the hell?* I jerked to a sitting position, my heart thundering in my chest while I looked around. My head was still thick with fog from my sleepy state. My muscles ached from the awkward position I'd drifted off in. After a few seconds, I realized the music was coming from the Hogues' patio speakers.

How can that be? The Hogues were long gone, and no one else was supposed to be here.

I shook away the fog in my brain and eased myself into a sitting position as a giant splash came from the pool right outside my window.

What the hell?

My heart jolted into my throat, and I shot forward onto my feet and into action. I snatched my phone off the coffee table and pulled up my employer's phone number. When I got to the front window that looked out at the pool, I slowly pulled down the wooden blind and peeked through it. All I could see was water splashing as a figure I couldn't make out swam across it.

My hands shook as I pushed the button to call Simon Hogue.

It might have been my safest bet to call 911, but it wasn't like someone was breaking into the pool house. They were just… swimming.

I released the blind and threw my back against the wall, rationalizing all the possibilities while the phone rang and rang. Perhaps Simon and Bridget had cut their vacation short. Maybe they'd given a neighbor permission to use the pool.

Neither of those options seemed likely. The Hogues would have informed me if they'd given someone permission to enter, and they certainly would have warned me that they were cutting their trip short.

I swallowed at the other possibility, the one I desperately

didn't want to believe. What if it was a complete stranger? Someone who had decided to take a late-night dip in a random pool, thinking that no one was home. The last thought brought a shiver up my spine.

When Simon's phone sent me to voicemail, I let out a frustrated groan. What options did I have? I could confront whoever was out there or flicker the lights to let them know someone was here. No, I couldn't do any of that. I would have to call 911. Before I could begin to dial the emergency number, my phone's screen lit up in my hands, and it started to vibrate, alerting me of a call coming through.

Pulling in a deep breath, I squeezed my eyes shut and tried to steady my nerves. I was being ridiculous. "Hey, Simon," I rushed. "There's—"

"Hiya, Chelsea," Simon started before I could even finish my sentence, seemingly unfazed by my panic. "How are you getting on? Good, I hope."

My eyes turned to the front window still masked by blinds. "Let's just say I'm glad you called. I know it's late where you are, but—" I swallowed, willing my nerves to settle so Simon could understand me. "You wouldn't happen to know who's swimming laps in your pool at this hour, would you?"

Simon's light chuckle sent a shot of relief through my veins. "That's just Liam, my late best friend's little brother."

Relief rushed through me the moment Simon identified the late-night swimmer by name.

Simon continued on. "There was—uh—a bit of an emergency back home. He had to get away quite abruptly and asked to stay at our place. We were just heading to bed, and I saw his message that he arrived unexpectedly early. I was hoping to warn you before you—"

"Called the cops?" I finished with a roll of my eyes. I was glad my employer couldn't see me, but a little warning would have been nice. "I'm glad you called me back. I didn't know what else to do."

Simon's laughter boomed through the line. "We'll be home next week, as planned. Liam will stay in the basement guest room of the main house, so he shouldn't be a bother. He'll surely keep to himself, but if you need anything, feel free to ring."

We said our goodbyes, and I hung up, annoyance replacing my relief. I'd chosen not to say anything to Simon about the rude way I had been woken up by his *friend*, but this Liam guy wasn't going to get off the hook that easily.

I opened the door and stepped out onto the patio to find Liam swimming laps across the water. He reached the opposite end, flipped around, kicked off the wall, and swam toward me. I stepped around the patio table and chairs to walk toward the edge of the pool. I waited for him to come up for air—to introduce myself and to kindly ask that he turn down the volume. Simon had mentioned this Liam guy was someone's *little* brother—but when my eyes registered the body that swam past the underwater pool lights, I realized I wasn't dealing with anyone little at all. Simon's friend's little brother, Liam, was very much a man.

Liam hadn't seen me, but I saw enough to know he was tall, lean, and sculpted. He cut through the water like an experienced swimmer, only popping his head up to sip the air before twisting back below the surface.

A knot twisted in my chest when my eyes skimmed the man's taut muscles as he pushed against the water with one fluid stroke then another. Every ridge and line of his back, arms, shoulders, and calves perfectly defined his strength. He swam another two laps, keeping his pace and taking sips of air so effortlessly I questioned if he had gills for lungs.

The man was an athlete, a beast underwater, and for the second time that day, I found myself transfixed by a stranger.

I stepped back slowly, suddenly anxious about interrupting his intense workout, but on my next step backward, I failed to remember the round table and chairs I'd skirted around to get to the pool. The back of my leg hit a chair, making it scrape across the travertine. When I reached back to catch my fall, I could find nothing to grip.

I landed hard on my ass, my palms slamming into the surface behind me. I howled at the pain that shot up my wrist. Of course, that caught Liam's attention. His head popped out from the water, and he swam toward the edge. He shot out of the pool so fast, I didn't even have time to react.

"Who's there?" he boomed like I was the one who'd just intruded on *his* peaceful night.

My defenses were on alert. I pushed my shoulders back as the pain in my wrist faded, and my chin tilted up as I prepared to let him have it. But then my eyes caught on the man's face, now illuminated in the dim orange patio lighting. It only took a second to realize we'd met before.

He was shirtless, dripping wet, with tattoos fully covering both arms, and his eyes were free of the dark shades that had hid them earlier—but I knew he was the same arrogant man who had passed me at Spill the Tea.

"Well, hello again, love." Liam flashed me a beaming smile, a wicked gleam in his beautiful green eyes. "Heading out for that proper shag I hope."

Shit.

3

LIAM

The poor love sat there, her emotions completely unmasked. Everything she felt was written across her beautiful face—confusion, intrigue, disappointment, more confusion, fear, anger.

It was the anger that gave me pause, that made me stare deeper, hoping the transparency she wore went beyond her glowing fair skin and silver-moon eyes. I wanted to know where that anger came from because I knew I couldn't take all the credit. She didn't even know me. Yet.

Perhaps I should have gone with a different greeting—one that didn't have to do with shagging some man with a giant knob—so I tried for something different to spark conversation. "You must be the nanny."

"And *you* must be the early arrival."

I bit down on my smile and reached out my hand to help her up, but she didn't take it. Instead, her eyes widened as they scrolled past my hands to my arms and traced the ink canvas.

I was intrigued by her reaction to me, both at the tearoom and again here. She gazed at me like I was half-man, half-alien, and a very strange part of me deep in my black heart felt a thrill from it. To have someone assess me like I was an actual stranger and not the public failure I'd become was refreshing, to say the least.

I didn't wait any longer for her to accept my help getting up. Instead, I wrapped my palm around her hand and lifted her until she was standing.

She was average height with a heart-shaped face and plump light-pink lips. Her copper hair was wavy, just hitting the top of her shoulders, and from that close up, I spotted a cluster of freckles on her cheeks.

I'd picked up on how gorgeous she was the first time I'd laid eyes on her in Spill the Tea, but it had been the spitfire conversation she'd been having with that Gwen woman that had caught my attention first.

"Chelsea, is it?" I remembered her name from earlier in the day, even though Simon had mentioned it too. I hadn't remembered much of what he'd told me about the live-in nanny other than that she was staying in their pool house and that I should leave her be. My mind snorted at the irony. I'd only been in America for a day, and I was already breaking rules. "I'm Liam."

Her eyes narrowed. "Yes, I'm aware of who you are *now*," she said as she pulled her hand out from mine. "Simon called. Good thing because I was about to call the cops."

The irritation in her tone answered my earlier question about where her anger was coming from. That was it. I'd frightened her. "Apologies. I didn't know anyone else was home."

"Well, I am." She folded her arms and tilted her head at me with a glare. "I'm here most of the time, so if you could keep the music down at night, that would be great."

I opened my mouth to point out that it was only eight

o'clock, hardly late, but that seemed to be missing her point. She was clearly perturbed that I was there in the first place. "I promise to keep the noise down."

As much as I wanted to say more—or to make some sort of deal about giving her what she wanted if she gave me what I wanted—I thought better of it. It was best for me to keep my mouth shut. The last thing I needed in my life was tension with this woman who I didn't even know. Enough strangers were angry at me back home.

After I had accepted the role on a reality television show cleverly titled *British Bachelor*, I had expected the aftermath to play out very differently than it had. During the entire promotional period and even during the first two months of the show airing, I was a god to the media. Even though I knew how the show would end, and that it would be disappointing at best, I had never expected the fallout to be so damaging. Clearly, I'd been in denial.

I'd fucked up, which wouldn't surprise most people who knew me, but this time I'd fucked up on a reality TV show that happened to have record-breaking ratings and an insane amount of buzz. According to executives, the show was going to resurrect me from "ex-Olympic athlete fame" to "influencer-level famous." While I could care less about using my brand to sell products for other companies, it was a start.

My mission had been simple. I would date a bunch of women, choose one at the end, and live a long and happy life shagging said woman. At thirty-three years old, I had no problem signing on to that plan—until it had come time to choose from my top three women. I'd never felt so trapped in my life, and I'd had no bloody clue how to handle it.

In the end, I'd walked away from all of them. I'd also walked away from a one-point-five-million-pound contract. Since I hadn't shown up to the show's finale, which consisted of a live interview between all the contestants and myself, I hadn't earned a single penny.

I could have coped with the financial disappointment. What I couldn't cope with was how explosive the media had become, which fed into the rabid fan base of the show, creating a shitstorm afterward.

My first reaction had been to flee. Simon's manor in Providence, Rhode Island, had seemed like the perfect destination. No one would know me there. Not yet, anyway. Things would change when the show's repeats started to play on American television, but I planned to be long gone before that time.

For the moment, all I wanted was some peace during my perfect little getaway so I could contemplate how to dig myself out of the hole I'd made. It was the only place I could think to go where I wouldn't be followed, photographed, or screamed at, and I intended to keep it that way. Which meant, other than Simon and Bridget, no one could know about my stint on reality television, including the nanny.

"Well, thank you." Chelsea stepped back, tension seeming to dissipate from her body. Her shoulders relaxed, and her narrowed eyes softened. Then she cleared her throat. "So, Liam. What brings you to Providence?"

"Holiday." The word came quickly, so quickly it sounded false even to me.

She quirked an eyebrow. "Without the Hogues here?"

I shrugged. "They will be."

"So you plan to stay awhile, then?"

"Oh, I don't know. Maybe a month."

That gave her pause. She shifted her stance, and I could almost guess the next question that would pop from her mouth.

"That's a long vacation. What is it you do for work?"

"I'm between contracts at the moment." I'd thought about

all of the one-off questions a stranger might ask me, but I hadn't expected them all at once. My plan was to be vague, charming, polite, and never give anyone reason to look me up on a search engine and find out the cold truth.

"What is your line of work?"

"I'm in the entertainment industry, but the details are all quite confidential." *Time to change the subject.* My first thought was to invite her for a swim, but then I remembered something. "I should be getting back to my swim. I don't want to keep you from your activities. You're off to a good shagging, is that right?"

Chelsea laughed lightly, and I detected discomfort there. I purposely kept my eyes on her skin, eagerly waiting for it to redden. I was rewarded with a deep-pink blush from her neck to her cheeks.

"Gwen finds too much pleasure in my personal life," Chelsea said. "She crossed the line today. I thought if I gave her something to talk about, she'd quit prying."

I bent my brows together. "So, I'm to believe you are *not* shagging a man with a giant willy?"

The smile she gave me next felt brighter than the pool's glow behind me. "I am not, indeed, shagging a man with a giant willy. Not tonight, anyway."

"That's unfortunate for you, I suppose."

Her eyes settled on mine, no longer narrowing in anger and no longer bent in confusion. She was looking at me like a woman who might just be flirting. While I knew I'd started it, I knew it was poor judgment to let it continue.

I slapped my palms to my sides. "Well, lovely chat. I've got to get back to my lengths." I laughed at the strange look she gave me. "Or I should say laps."

She took a step back toward the pool house. "I hope you enjoy your stay. If you have trouble finding anything, just knock or use the intercom system. I know my way around the manor pretty well, so…" Her voice trailed off as her gaze slipped back down my body.

Her wandering eyes made me want to show her exactly what heaven was made of. But the second my thoughts started to go there, down their naturally dark and dirty path, I stopped myself. This trip wasn't about wetting my knob, though I could have gone for a good shag after months of celibacy. I had a plan, and I would stick to it.

I'd given myself some hard rules to follow before calling Simon and jumping on that plane for America. Number one, no social media. I had deactivated all my accounts in an effort to go completely silent. Number two, no sex. Not until I'd cleaned up my mess back home. Number three, I would give myself one month. I couldn't hide out forever. In one month's time, I would go home and face the music. If the public still wanted to shame and hate me for doing what I felt was right, then so be it. I would at least face their wrath with a clear head and a full heart.

But as Chelsea and I parted—her closing the pool house door behind her and me heading toward the remote that controlled the surround sound before diving back into the pool—I knew I was in trouble. Maybe more trouble than I'd left back home.

It was only day one, and my self-imposed rules were already hard to follow. I couldn't think about all the hard endeavors to come.

4

CHELSEA

I t was noon when I grabbed the Hogues' mail then
crossed the rear courtyard terrace to enter the back
entrance of their main house. The double French doors
led directly into the dining room and open kitchen. I set the
mail down on the square granite island and found a large jug
from the cabinets. After filling it to the brim with water, I
started my daily rounds of watering the indoor plants. It was
the only time I had reason to enter the main home, and I was
strangely aware of the fact that there was a man in the house
with me today. If I was quick and quiet, I could probably
make it out before he saw me.

Last night had been awkward. I couldn't imagine how
much more awkward things would have been if Simon hadn't
called me back when he did. The cops would have arrived.
The neighbors would have freaked out. The Hogues would
have had to call to clear up the entire mess. And Liam would
have been caught in the middle of it all, making for a shitty
holiday for him.

A little more notice from the Hogues would have been

great, but in retrospect, everything was fine. I just needed to do what I came to do and retire to my pool house to work on my book.

My book. That was where my focus should be. I'd finally worked up the nerve to contact a list of editors I'd been keeping. One of them had immediate availability, which I quickly learned was rare. My plan was to take one more pass at my manuscript then send it out before I could lose my nerve.

I didn't need any more reason to dwell on quitting school, not when my love for the written word rose above anything any professor could ever teach me. Creativity didn't come from acquiring a degree or having anyone *approve* my art. It came from living, from breathing, and expressing.

The classroom would never teach me what life could— what a real job would. Experience was what I needed to feed my creativity. I'd already trusted that bold voice in my head that would never shut up. Now, I just had to be bold enough to publish.

Sighing, I climbed the ladder of Simon's library bookshelf to reach a succulent that sat in the windowsill above, a cactus that I was only required to water once that week. It was a bulb-shaped thing with spines blossoming every which way. I checked the soil and confirmed it was dry before soaking it thoroughly, just as instructed.

"Hello, love."

The deep voice bulleted through the air so unexpectedly that I jumped and turned toward it. My movements were too fast. I lost my grip on the ladder and reached back for it but missed, cupping the cactus instead.

"Ah!" I screamed as the damn spines pierced my skin.

I fell backward, imagining my deathly tumble to the hard-wood ten feet below. Luckily, strong arms caught me instead, and he made the catch feel effortless.

I opened my eyes, my heart pounding a million miles a second, and sucked in a breath when I found Liam staring down at me. His green eyes sparkled, reminding me of the first time I saw moss on a tree. My parents had taken me to George Washington State Campground for a weekend getaway when I was a little girl. We set up a tent, fished in the lake, and hiked for miles. There was nothing like the feeling of nature surrounding me, and I was completely in awe. Everything felt bigger than life, just like the man standing in front of me now.

"I frightened you again, didn't I?" His smile faded, but he made no move to set me down.

The burning sensation in my hand intensified, drawing my attention to where the cactus had pierced my skin. *Holy shit. The pain.* I held my hand up, almost afraid to see the damage. Three of the needles were still wedged in my palm. Just the sight of them made it hurt more.

"What the—" Liam's eyes widened as he took in my injury, then he sprang into action. Everything happened so fast. He jogged, carrying me to the couch, and set me down. He grabbed my injured hand and examined it, flipping it over, bringing it closer to him, all with a gentle touch. One by one, he carefully plucked the long spines from my fingers.

Even after my hands were free and clear of cactus needles, the burning continued to intensify, spreading from my wounds to every inch of my body, including my neck and face. Within seconds, I could see bumps rising on my skin. "Are those hives?" I squealed.

Liam scanned my arms then my face and confirmed it with a nod. "Afraid so, sweetheart. Stay here. I'll fetch some medicine." He started to jog away then halted before spinning around to face me. "Do you happen to know where I can find some?"

"In the hall bathroom upstairs next to the girls' room."

He took off. I didn't know for how long. All I knew was that my body felt on fire and that it itched just as badly as it burned. The bumps were everywhere that I could see, and I felt lightheaded.

When Liam finally returned, it was with a bottle of medicine. "Take this," he said as he uncapped the bottle and poured a dose of it into a plastic measuring cup. "You might feel drowsy after, but it will make the hives go away."

I didn't hesitate. I drank down the nasty syrup in one gulp and handed him the cup before rising to my feet. "I should get back to my place."

Liam stood, towering over me and bunching his brows together. Until that moment, I couldn't have imagined an angry Liam. Cocky, definitely. Annoyingly witty, for sure. But angry, no.

"You're not going anywhere, not until those hives go away." He pointed to the couch. "Lie down."

I let out a laugh. He was being ridiculous. "I'll be fine, Liam. I'd rather rest at my place."

"Then I'm coming with you until you feel better."

"What? No."

He narrowed his eyes. "I'm not a doctor, and I just administered medicine to you. I'd like to make sure you don't go into some sort of anaphylactic shock."

Squeezing my lids together, I slapped my hands to my sides and shrugged. "Fine. Whatever. But I need to finish watering the plants."

"Rest first. The plants can wait."

I found something deeply sexy about his commanding tone, especially since it was with the intention of helping me heal. For that reason alone, I gave in, turned away, and walked back to the pool house with Liam right behind me.

By the time we walked into my place, I was dizzy with exhaustion. If he weren't with me, I would have gone straight to my bedroom, shut all my curtains, and crawled under the covers. But I couldn't bring Liam to my room. I didn't even know the guy. I did feel some peace knowing he was a close friend of the Hogues', but still. He was a stranger. The fact that I'd seen him with his shirt off and that he'd just saved my life didn't matter.

He closed the door behind us, and I turned around to give him one more chance to escape.

"You really don't have to stay. I'll be fine." I was less insistent this time, already resigned to the fact that he wouldn't listen to me. He seemed like a stubborn man.

"I'm staying, Chelsea."

A wave of exhaustion rolled over me. I was done arguing. "Fine."

I lay down on my couch and dragged my chunky gray knit throw blanket over me. The next thing I knew, my lids were growing heavy. Soon, I would be fast asleep. With a British stranger taking a seat on the chair across from me.

5

LIAM

The moment Chelsea's breathing deepened, I picked her up and brought her to her bed, where I knew she would be more comfortable. It was a small room with just enough space for a queen bed and a small closet, nothing more. Tiptoeing out of the room, I left the door ajar and walked out into the main room complete with a living room and kitchenette.

At first, I paced around her place, contemplating what to do with my time. I understood how creepy that could seem to the average person, but I also didn't know what I would do if her reaction worsened in my absence. With me keeping an eye on her, I could drive her to the hospital if it came to that. I didn't think it would, but I also wasn't a doctor, and I didn't know why her body had reacted so harshly to a cactus.

Call Simon, my inner voice urged me a second later. I contemplated it only because I didn't want to worry him and Bridget while they were on vacation. It would be early morning back in London, so I sent him a text message instead.

Liam: *Not an emergency. The nanny stuck herself with a cactus and broke out in hives. She took some Benadryl and passed out. What do you think, doc?*

A second later, my phone rang, and Simon's name popped up on the caller ID. "Hiya, Simon."

"What in the bloody hell, Liam? What happened?"

I was careful to keep my voice low so as not to wake Chelsea. "She was watering your succulents." I skipped the part about spooking her a little when I came into the study and making her fall from the ladder. "And she managed to get stuck by a cactus. She broke out in hives, and I didn't know what to do, so I gave her Benadryl."

"Bollocks," Simon muttered under his breath. "When did you administer the antihistamine?"

I thought about it for a second. "About thirty minutes ago."

"The hives should have faded mostly by now. Have they?"

"I can check." I walked back into Chelsea's bedroom and slid to the side she was facing. Her face was completely flawless, like a porcelain doll I dared not touch. Her chest rose with her steady breathing, slow and deep, just a light whistle of noise with her exhale. She looked completely perfect, like nothing had happened at all.

"All clear, doc," I whispered before slipping back out of her room.

"Glad to hear it. You did well, but next time, maybe you should call me before you decide to play doctor with the nanny."

The mental image that came to mind when Simon uttered the words "play doctor with the nanny" probably wasn't what he was referring to, but I didn't hate the visual it conjured up. "Right," I said, clearing my throat. "Will do."

"How are you getting on at the house? Finding everything you need?"

And just like that, my thoughts whiplashed from Chelsea in a short white button-up dress to the gratitude I felt toward Simon and his wife for taking me in so abruptly, no explanations necessary. "All good. You have a beautiful home, Simon. Thank you again for letting me stay. I'll be out of your hair as soon as I figure out how to deal with this whole mess."

"No rush. We have plenty of room, and it will be nice to catch up once we're home."

We ended the chat, and I stuck my phone in my back pocket while perusing her small stack of books on a narrow shelf. I plucked one at random to take a closer look. The cover was a black-and-white photo of half of a man's face staring back at me. Music notes and faded lyrics added to the background. The title, in bold yellow script, read *Dangerous Hearts*. Curious, I thumbed about halfway through the book and started reading.

Letting out a ragged breath, I slip my finger beneath the fabric of her shorts until it meets her pussy. So perfect. So wet. Already.

Fuck. My eyes immediately bulged at the erotic words. Shaking my head, I focused on the passage again and continued reading.

I glide my finger up and down at a tortuously slow pace, giving her every chance in the world to refuse me. Her legs slide open, her clit swelling beneath my touch. I still make no move to take the plunge, not yet, although I know it's what she wants.

I let her shift a bit more. She's practically begging for it, and it's hot as hell, but if this is really happening, I'm going to make it last as long as possible. Lyric deserves the VIP treatment, multiple orgasms initiated by intense and mind-blowing foreplay. She'll be screaming when she comes in my mouth, but only when I'm ready to let her.

My finger slips back down her leg, drawing a wet line on her skin. Reaching for the band of her shorts, I swiftly remove them, revealing the finest ass I've ever seen. It's round and firm, sitting perfectly below her tiny waist.

Just staring at Lyric's curves is enough to get me off. Seeing her bare is more arousing than I was ready for. I pull my erection from my shorts and tug at it a few times, hoping to relieve some of the pressure. To my surprise, Lyric takes that moment to look at me over her shoulder, her eyes darkening by the second. I squeeze her ass and watch as her teeth sink into her plush bottom lip. I fucking lose it.

I shift her so her legs are on either side of mine and my feet are angled to lock her body in place. She's still lying flat on her stomach, and I'm sitting with my back resting against the headboard, but now her clit is directly below my cock, right where I want it. With her eyes still on me, I stick a finger in my mouth and suck, giving her an idea of what I'm about to do. I grin and sink it straight into her wet opening until her eyes roll back in her head.

Hell yes. So warm and soft but tight. So tight. My dick throbs knowing those narrow walls will be wrapped around me soon. I don't know if I can resist much longer, not after feeling what's waiting for me.

My free hand palms one of her ass cheeks, gripping it for leverage as I sink and twist and jerk my finger in her depths. My hands are big, and one finger is enough for someone as tight as Lyric, but if I'm going to prepare her for taking all of me, she needs to understand what she's in for. So I dip a second finger into her tightness and then a third. She screams a little. It's a quiet scream but a scream none the less. I smile in victory while continuing to pump until her walls begin to strangle me. She's so close.

Call me a savage beast, but I won't let her come yet. That was just a primer. I withdraw my fingers, and she mewls in disappointment.

Holy shit. I set the book on the couch's armrest and adjusted my trousers a touch to keep myself together. I was as hard as a fucking rock, and my heart was hammering from what I'd just read. I didn't know much about Chelsea, but I sure liked what I knew—her smut emporium of reading material shooting straight to the top of that list.

I cleared my throat, forcing my thoughts on something less erotic in an effort to calm the beast in my trousers. I would have to take care of myself later. Against my better judgment, I plucked the *Dangerous Heart* book from the armrest, stuck it inside my waistband, and pulled my shirt over it. I would just borrow it for a short while, then I would return it when she wasn't looking. Harmless. At least that was the intention.

It was an hour later when I heard Chelsea's breathing change, and I stood up to check on her for the billionth time. She was sitting up in bed, her hair tossed about and her tank twisted enough that I caught some side boob before she righted it and squinted back at me.

"You're still here."

I couldn't tell if it was surprise or relief that filled her tone, but I was happy it wasn't disappointment. "How do you feel?"

She stretched, revealing her midriff as her shirt lifted with her arms. "A little foggy but better, I think."

"You look better." I caught my words and realized how she could interpret them the wrong way. "I mean, the hives are gone. You're on the mend."

She blew out a breath of relief. "Thank you for the rescue back there. If it weren't for your heroic catch, I would have ended up with broken bones too."

"It was nothing." I took a step back, suddenly feeling like an intruder. I had no reason to linger, and I definitely shouldn't have borrowed her book without permission. "I'll be on my way. If you need anything, you know where to find me."

I'd already made it halfway to the front door when Chelsea called to me. "Wait, um."

I turned to see her rush out from her room, eyes wide as they fixed on me.

"Let me repay you with lunch. You've got to be hungry."

I hadn't even thought about lunch until she mentioned it. My stomach answered her with a rumble I knew she couldn't hear. Lunch with the nanny—while it sounded appealing, it also sounded like a terrible idea. When I didn't answer right away, she continued.

"We could go somewhere, or I could make something here." She looked toward her kitchen. "I think I have some bread and cold cuts in the fridge."

I made a face I knew could be taken as rude, but I couldn't help myself. "Sarnies are much better here in America, I suppose, but—" I was going to give her some lie about needing to run an errand instead of joining her for lunch when I caught the anxious look in her eyes. The look told me I would crush her feelings if I didn't allow her to return whatever favor it was she thought she owed me. "We can go somewhere, if that's all right with you. Perhaps I should get to know the area a little while we're out."

Chelsea let out a smile, and she almost looked relieved. "Okay, let me just get dressed."

"Of course."

She rushed back into her room then shut the door behind her.

While she was changing, I made a mad dash to her small shelf and pulled her book I'd borrowed from my trousers. Sweat would surely ruin her precious book if I didn't put it back, and guilt still gnawed at me for taking it to begin with.

I'd just slipped the book back into its rightful position on the shelf when I heard a sound I should have detected sooner. I hadn't noticed the door behind me open until it was too late.

"What are you doing?"

Shit. Chelsea's voice was dangerously low and suspicious. I whipped my head around to face her, almost afraid to find what was staring back at me. How much had she seen? Maybe she hadn't seen me pull the book of word porn from my trousers.

"Why were you pulling my book from your underwear?"

Double shit. I held up my hands in defense, like that could protect me from whatever wrath came with sticking my nose where it didn't belong. "I'm fascinated by your—" I waved at the shelf behind me, not knowing what to call it. "Taste in books. Nice library."

She stepped closer, getting a look at the book I'd just had in my hands. Her eyes lit up with amusement. "Did you read any of it, or did you just like the cover?"

I twisted my mouth and bent my brows together at her question. "You were asleep for quite some time, and these were on display." I waved my hand toward her shelves. "Trust me, I had no idea I'd be entertaining myself with such titillating content." Turning the tables had never felt so good.

Now it was Chelsea's turn to look shocked. "I don't know what's worse, that you stole my book or that you actually wanted to read it."

I chuckled, pleased to see this lighthearted side of her. It was good to know she wasn't always so uptight. "I was curious, mostly."

"Curious?" She studied my face like she could find more to my admission there. "About the book or me?"

"Both, I suppose."

She stepped forward until she was right in front of me, and a spark of hope ignited in my chest, a spark that I knew better than to let burn. I imagined Chelsea leaning in and giving me a taste of those full pink lips. I imagined her chest brushing mine and the soft caress of her fingers running over my biceps. It was only a flash, but it was vivid enough I inhaled sharply.

I hadn't seen her reach past me, but when she pulled back and smacked something against my chest, I didn't have to look down to know what it was. "Books are meant to be shared. Just make sure to return it when you're done."

With a wink, she turned away, and that was the moment I knew Chelsea would test my limits, limits I couldn't afford to exceed.

6

CHELSEA

It was only a ten-minute ride from the Hogues' manor to downtown Providence, and in that short time, I learned three interesting facts about Liam. The man didn't appear to be addicted to electronics like the rest of mankind. Not once did he reach for his phone—he'd said he called Simon earlier, so I knew he had one on him. For an instant, I wondered if that was a British thing, then I had a flashback to my interview with the Hogues and how many times Simon had to ask me to repeat a response to a question because he was constantly staring down at his device.

We shared similar taste in music. Seconds after getting into my old red Honda Accord, Liam managed to find a Panic at the Disco CD and started playing it. Not only that but he mouthed the words, not messing up a single lyric as he went. I would be lying if I said the perfect synchronization of his lips to the words didn't intrigue me.

He was a stranger, but he didn't feel like one. I found something comforting about his presence when nothing had felt comfortable at all lately. Perhaps it was the calm that surrounded him, even in our most awkward meetings. Maybe it was that crooked hint of a smile that never seemed to leave his face. Maybe the fact that he was a stranger was what comforted me most of all.

In all my years living in Providence, I'd been surrounded by the same friends, family, and schoolmates. It was like a little bubble that had, in ways, sheltered me from the outside world, and it was only now that I was beginning to realize how isolated my life had been.

My parents had never taken me on any big vacations, mostly because they felt like I should be in school or they were taking an anniversary trip and wanted to be alone. While my parents loved me plenty, I knew that if I wanted adventure, I would have to make my own. *One day I will*, I kept telling myself.

I parked along the curb on Westminster Street in front of a row of restaurants. "We're here," I sang out and exited my car. When I reached the sidewalk, Liam was already outside spinning slowly on his heels and taking in the sights.

I was aware of the pleasing aesthetics the bustling cityscape held. Set upon the walkable riverfront at Waterplace Park, historic landmarks, and flourishing greenery, my city was as beautiful as it got in the US, and Liam appeared to recognize that.

"You okay there, buddy?" I teased as his gaze wandered over the dome-shaped architecture of the state capitol building.

He turned his head toward me, his brows bunching in the middle. "Yeah, why?"

I bit the inside of my lip. "You look like Ariel from *The Little Mermaid* when she poked her head out from under the sea."

He shook his head as if to say he didn't understand the reference.

My jaw dropped. "You've never seen *The Little Mermaid?* The story of the mermaid who made a deal with the sea witch to give up her voice so she could turn into a human and fall in love with the hunky prince?" I laughed at my description of my favorite Disney movie. When Liam still looked confused, I shook my head and placed my hands on my hips. "Well, that's disappointing."

"If this movie is anything like your book collection, I'm happy to try it out." His crooked smile broadened, creating a flurry of activity in my chest.

With a roll of my eyes, I placed a palm at his back and nudged him forward. "Forget I said anything."

We walked while I pointed out each restaurant and gave him an idea of what he would find on the menu, but he shook his head at everything until we arrived at a coal-fired pizza joint on Westminster Street.

"Good choice." I smiled and walked through the door he held open for me.

I was in heaven the second he opened the door. The corner building was brightly lit and spacious, with fresh Italian seasonings scenting the air. It was one of my favorite places in all of Providence to go for lunch. So much so that I used to bring my homework and request a quiet spot in the corner where I would sit for hours.

"How about a booth over there?" I suggested to Liam.

He just nodded casually, and I turned to smile at the woman standing at the host stand. The woman nodded to my request and showed us to our table.

Liam ordered a beer, and I asked for their house pinot grigio. Once our waitress was gone, I started to worry Liam and I wouldn't have anything to talk about. It wasn't like me to invite strangers to lunch. Especially mysterious strangers from foreign countries. And I hoped he wouldn't assume there was more behind my invitation.

"So, Chelsea..." He hesitated, and I assumed he was reaching for my last name.

"Banks."

The corner of his mouth tipped up in a smile. "Cute."

My cheeks heated, and I didn't know why. Clearly, Liam was a flirt. I also got the impression that he was trouble, and I didn't just get that impression from his ink-covered arms and that cocky smile he loved to use. The fact that he'd come to stay at Simon and Bridget's without them being home said a lot. It said that he'd been in a hurry and couldn't wait another week for them to arrive. But why? Had he done something? Was someone trying to hurt him? Crazy thoughts raced through my mind until he spoke again.

"So, Chelsea Banks, certainly nannying doesn't take up all your time. Are you in school?"

"I was." I debated how much I should tell him in those next few moments of silence then realized I had nothing to lose telling a stranger the truth. He wouldn't be sticking around much longer, and it would feel nice to just talk about it for once. "I was in the middle of obtaining my doctorate when I dropped out a couple months ago."

Liam's brows ticked up with curiosity. "This sounds like an interesting story."

I felt my cheeks heat again. "It's not that interesting. I was good at school, and I kept at it because I thought eventually I'd figure out what I wanted to do with my degrees. Since I was a little girl, I've wanted to work with kids as an educator in some fashion. But when I started taking the classes, I realized I didn't want to be stuck in a classroom all day. So I kept trying to figure out what direction I should take until I realized education wasn't what I wanted to do at all."

"But you still want to nanny?"

I nodded without an ounce of hesitation. The one thing I knew I was doing right with my time was caring for the Hogues' kids. "Yes, definitely. It's one of those jobs that doesn't feel like work to me at all. I've gotten quite attached to those kids in just a couple of months, and it leaves me time to work on other things."

"Like?"

I didn't mind telling Liam about dropping out of school, but I felt a little queasy at the thought of confessing my passion for writing. "I dabble in the arts. In, um, writing."

"What do you write?"

His question was so simple, yet it only pulled me deeper into the dark bubble I'd holed up in ever since I'd drafted my first book. I was days away from sending it to my editor. With zero books published and a new idea for a story currently running rampant in my mind, it all just felt like a silly dream, one I had no idea on earth how to make come true.

"You know what? It's all very new, and I'm not ready to talk about it, if that's okay."

He didn't pry. He didn't make me feel bad about objecting to sharing. He simply shrugged and leaned back in his seat before grabbing the menu and checking out the options. I let out a long, slow breath, feeling grateful for the reprieve, knowing I couldn't go my entire life avoiding the conversation. Not only did I fear my own dreams, but I feared what would happen if I continued to keep silent.

"So, you're the best friend's little brother?" I asked with a smile, trying desperately to find a new topic of conversation.

Liam lifted his eyes from the menu and nodded. "That's me. Simon and my brother, Blake, were very close."

Confusion twisted my features. "Were? Is that not the case anymore?" I hoped I didn't sound like I was prying.

Liam set down his menu, his eyes softening. "Blake died in a horrible boating accident years ago. Simon was with him when it happened. I was fourteen."

Dread sank into my gut. "I'm so sorry to hear that. I didn't know."

"Of course you didn't." Liam picked up his menu again and returned to scanning it.

Once again, I was at a loss for conversation, but my eyes were still curious as they traveled the length of his arm. The intricate designs seemed to blend together, but the closer I looked, the more I understood where one tattoo ended and another began. Suddenly, I wished I could go back in time and get another glimpse of Liam's bare skin. I would pay more attention to the art, to what each piece looked like. Maybe I would learn a bit more about the mystery that was Liam, whose last name I still did not know. Then my eyes caught on his brother's name written in script font on his bicep.

"Who designed your tattoos?"

Liam's sideways grin appeared again, allowing me to breathe a bit easier. I was back in safe conversation territory. "Me. I dabble in the arts too."

And with that fact, I might have developed a bit of a crush on the boy from the other side of the pond.

"Do you have any?" he asked without looking up.

I was still pondering my new crush when he asked the question. It took me a minute to realize what he was asking. "Um, oh." He was talking about tattoos. "No, not yet. I haven't figured out what I'd want to commit to forever."

He nodded. "I guess it's a big decision."

"Wasn't it for you?"

He thought about my question for a second, then he shook his head. "Nah. Ink might be the only form of commitment I'm okay with." Then he shrugged and quirked his lips before adopting an embellished Jersey accent. "That's my credo. No ragrets."

I bit back a smile. "You have no regrets? Like not even a single letter?"

We both laughed at the reference to *We're the Millers*, but in the back of my mind, his comment about commitment rang loud and clear. Red flags waved in front of my face, and I knew I couldn't entertain my crush on the hot British stranger sitting across from me for another second.

"Maybe I can draw you something, and we can face your fear of commitment together."

He winked, catching my heart completely off guard. I wasn't expecting those eyes to pierce me so deeply or his gesture to create such a visceral reaction in my chest. I laughed over my discomfort. "No offense, clearly you're a talented artist, but you don't know me well enough to create something that will be etched in my skin forever."

His smile softened while his eyes shone brighter. "Not yet, Chelsea Banks, but give me one week." He peered down at his menu while he mumbled his next words a little softer, "And I will."

7

LIAM

A door slammed in my dreams, causing my eyes to fly open and my heart to gallop to life. I awoke to the vision of Chelsea in my head, an ache at my groin, sheets around my feet, and my fist wrapped around my cock. I was already in midstroke before I realized what was happening. Sweat beaded on my skin as I worked furiously to release the buildup that suddenly felt excruciating.

I'd been dreaming about the nanny. Full lips, petite height, slim waist, curvy hips. Sure, she was sexy as hell, but she was nothing like the women I went for back home. Chelsea was as pure as they came. She had an innocent outlook, flawless skin, natural everything. But she made me laugh, and I liked the sound of hers.

It wasn't until my release shot off in a powerful surge that I let out a heavy breath, bringing a wave of relaxation with it. I'd needed that. After everything I'd been through over the last two months, the past two weeks especially, that was the first time I'd truly let go. The burden of breaking the hearts of three women on a single day, all who had confessed to falling in love with me, still ate me up at night. But how was I to know I wouldn't fall in love with any of them?

"Afraid of commitment" and "the Forever Bachelor" were how the fans of the reality show had labeled me. Maybe they were right. Perhaps I was doomed to live as a single bloke after all.

I shook my head and groaned while stretching out my body. My eyes caught on the digital clock at my bedside, and I cursed. It was already noon. I'd been sleeping the day away without even realizing it. Still, I was groggy as fuck. With a plan to remedy that, I hopped out of bed, brushed my teeth, and quickly rinsed off in the shower. Once clean, I slipped on my swim shorts and headed out the back door to the courtyard.

The second I left the house, I could hear splashing and laughing above the surround sound, but I couldn't see a bloody thing. The area where Chelsea lived was fairly private with tall shrubs and trees surrounding the gate. I couldn't even get a glimpse of the area from the house, which I had attempted to do yesterday morning before she showed up to water the plants.

Once I reached the gate entrance and pushed my way inside, I halted completely in my steps. "Oh, shit."

Chelsea was climbing out of the pool in a hot yellow bikini, her firm bum prominently displayed. She paused at the sound of my voice and snapped her head in my direction. That was when I caught movement from inside the pool. Another woman with a similar bikini style lounged on a large watermelon floatation device with her shades on and her skin glistening.

"Well hey there," the unknown woman said with a slow-spreading grin.

I lifted my hand in a friendly wave. "Hiya. Apologies, loves. I didn't know the pool was reserved for the afternoon."

Chelsea stepped the rest of the way out of the pool and reached for a beach towel that sat on the lounge chair closest to her. "Morning, sleeping beauty," she said, her gaze traveling slowly over my body.

I pinched my brows together, happy that my shades hid my amusement. "How did you know I was sleeping?"

Her lips twitched, and her cheeks darkened in color, causing a heavy feeling to hit my gut. I remembered the sound of a door slamming when I woke up to find I was giving myself a good wank. Maybe Chelsea had been inside the house. Maybe she'd caught a glimpse of me. The possibility excited me far too much.

Then she shrugged and pointed to my head as she stopped in front of me. "Your hair. You must have been having a good dream."

Bloody hell, the minx had been there watching me. Too bad she'd left before it got good. "My dreams were excellent, thank you. Would you like to hear about one?"

She let out an airy laugh, and I swore her cheeks pinkened even more. "Maybe some other time." She waved over the pool. "You're welcome to join us. There's room for everyone. That's my best friend, Maisey."

"Hello," I called out to her friend with a short wave.

"Hey there, Liam. I've heard lovely things about you."

Chelsea rolled her eyes and shook her head. "Don't believe her. I didn't say much other than that you saved my life and paid for lunch when it was supposed to be my treat. Oh." She snapped her fingers as if she'd remembered something else. "And that you're an artist."

She dropped her towel back on her chair and walked away from me. I followed her, not knowing where she was going, but

I didn't care much as my eyes fell to that glorious arse. When she stopped at a blue cooler and bent over to grab two beers from it, I wished I'd looked away sooner. The fabric of my trunks twitched with excitement. Then Chelsea whipped back around, handing me a beer. My eyes snapped up to hers a second too late.

"Thirsty?"

She was clearly referring to the beer, but that wasn't what I was thirsty for, not after watching her strut around the pool soaking wet and confident as hell. When I didn't say anything, Maisey let out a laugh.

"I'd say he's thirsty all right, darlin'. Go ahead. Give him a taste."

I choked on my next words but was saved by the sight of the door to Chelsea's pool house opening followed by a tall black man emerging. He caught sight of me and greeted me with a "Sup" and an uptick of his head.

My first thought was that this was the man whose willy Chelsea was going on about at the tearoom the other day. My chest tightened, and my jaw ticked with jealousy. I couldn't possibly feel possessive over a woman I barely knew, but she'd said there was no willy, that it had just been a ruse for Gwen's benefit.

My cautious eyes tracked the man as he strutted by us. I half expected him to stop in front of Chelsea, but he didn't even slow his steps before he dove into the pool. When he swam up beside Maisey and planted a fat kiss on her mouth, I swore my entire body exhaled.

I turned back to Chelsea to find her watching me with an amused purse of her lips. "That's Maisey's husband, Roger."

Swallowing, I shrugged my shoulder to tell Chelsea the information didn't serve me in the slightest. "Very well."

Chelsea's laughter was light. "You sure? Because you looked worried for a minute there."

I tilted my head and pulled my sunglasses from my head. "Did I? I can't imagine why."

She mocked me with a shrug of her own, the playful smile never leaving her gorgeous face. "If you say so." Then she brushed past me, her plump arse barely gliding against my front, and took a seat on a lounge chair.

Chelsea looked to be in her own world as she picked up a blue notebook and pen that sat beside her. A moment later, she was scribbling away like she'd been struck with a story idea.

I dove into the pool, careful to stay away from Chelsea's friends, who were making out in the shallow end, and swam enough lengths for my lungs to feel like they were bursting.

I pushed myself out of the water and sat on the edge, trying to catch my breath. When I looked up, I found all three pairs of eyes on me. Roger pointed a finger at me, and for a second, I thought he might have recognized me from *British Bachelor*.

"Dude. You're Liam Colborn."

Shit. Just like that, my pounding heart sank with the weight of being found out. "Um," I started, my eyes darting to Chelsea. *How am I going to explain this one to her without her hating me just like the others?*

Roger's eyes widened when he realized he was correct. "It *is* you."

He stood up straight and pointed his finger at me again. I didn't know if the finger-pointing gesture was an American thing, but it felt bloody rude.

Then Roger's booming voice started up again. "Eight-time individual gold medalist in two summer Olympics, not to mention a shit ton of group medals. Dude, I was obsessed with your career back in the day. What the hell happened to you?"

Laughter escaped my throat as relief flooded my veins. I found myself pleasantly surprised to be recognized for something other than being a playboy reality star. Lifting my hands and shoulders, I grinned. "I timed out, I guess. Two Olympics were plenty enough for me. I didn't think anyone would remember that." I flashed him a smile.

"You were ridiculous in the water. *You* are the reason I took up swimming in high school. I wanted to be you, man."

"Thank you, mate." While his comments were flattering, they were starting to make me feel old. Roger couldn't be more than four years younger than I. I had only been sixteen at my first Olympic swim meet, but so much time had passed since then.

"I just knew it was you when you started swimming those laps." Roger glanced between Chelsea and me, appearing confused. "Are you friends with Chelsea? How have we not met until now?"

I saw Chelsea watching us in my peripheral, and when Roger called her out, she stepped forward to the edge of the pool before sitting and sticking her legs in. "He's a friend of Simon's, his houseguest." Chelsea turned to me. "Don't mind Roger. He's a little obsessive when it comes to water sports."

"Ah, shit," Maisey said as she pulled herself up to sit on her raft. "I hate to ruin the party, but Roger and I have to go." She turned to Roger. "We have to leave soon to meet your parents at the yacht club."

Maisey exited the pool first, and Roger followed her. They disappeared into Chelsea's pool house, then it was just the woman in the yellow bikini and me.

"Working on your tan?" I called from across the pool.

She smiled and slipped into the pool. "Something like that."

I sank back into the water, too, keeping my distance so we were still at completely different ends. "I was thinking," I said, moving toward my beer waiting for me at the edge of the pool. "If I'm going to draw you some body art, I should get to know you a wee bit better."

Chelsea walked her way to the four-foot section of the pool, leaving a foot of her above the water to where I could just see the top of her cleavage. "That sounds a bit one-sided if you ask me."

"Well, you're not making me body art, now are you?"

"I could."

I chuckled. "I'm afraid I wouldn't let you draw my art if my life depended on it."

She grinned. "Fine, but I won't give up information freely. For everything you learn about me, you have to tell me something about you."

That plan didn't sound entirely threatening, though I wasn't thinking straight at the sight of her, especially when it was still in the back of mind that she could have seen me wanking off earlier. "Deal."

"Yeah?" Her eyes lit up as she stepped toward me in the pool.

It was instinct that made me meet her in the middle. "Yeah," I said. "Let's start now." She was an inch in front of me, her head only reaching my chest, and I had the strong desire to lift her tight body and wrap those slim legs around my waist. "First question," I said instead. "What were you writing in that notebook of yours?"

I loved that her face flushed every time I asked her something personal.

"I told you I like to write."

"Yes. But you didn't tell me *what* you like to write."

"Does it matter?"

I shrugged. "Depends if you want a tattoo of the Cat in the Hat or Fabio."

She laughed hard and deep, and I couldn't help but notice the way her entire face lit up with it. "Funny," she finally said. "But…" She seemed to think twice about what she was going to say before finally spitting out, "It would be closer to the Fabio version, I suppose."

My jaw fell open. I was half-shocked that she actually admitted that to me and half-amused that the nanny was spending her free time conjuring up sex scenes.

"Like that book you let me borrow, *Dangerous Hearts*?"

"Similar but different."

I chuckled. "You write porn."

Her hand flew out and smacked me in the arm. "No, I do not write porn. I write romance, love stories with steamy situations that move the story along. Nothing gratuitous, I assure you."

My grin stretched with her words. "Steamy situations?"

Her cheeks turned a deeper shade of red. "Never mind. Can we change the subject? Or swim? Isn't that what you came here to do?"

I shrugged. "I got my laps in. Now I'm just here to hang out with you."

She rolled her eyes. "Charming. But I'm getting out of the water."

With that, Chelsea pushed up over the edge, giving me a nice view of her arse once more. I didn't want to look away, but when I heard the door to Chelsea's pool house open, I averted my gaze so fast that I got a wee bit dizzy.

"We're out of here," Maisey called before hugging her friend. "Lunch later this week?"

Chelsea nodded then leaned in to hug Roger too. For the second time that day, I was jealous of the bloke who got to touch her, especially when she was wearing close to nothing.

"Nice to meet you," Maisey said to me.

I waved them both off and let out a little sigh of relief when they were gone. Alone at last. Not that I could do anything about it. I cursed under my breath as I watched Chelsea sit back down and prop her notebook on her lap.

I pushed myself out of the pool and casually strolled to the seat beside Chelsea.

She threw her towel onto it. "Seat's taken."

Laughing, I walked around to the chair on the other side of her.

"That one is taken too."

"What?" I laughed again, this time incredulously.

She peered over her shades. "I'm working, and you're distracting me."

I placed my hands on my hips. "How so?"

It was an invitation for her to look. I knew I had a good body. I worked hard to stay fit. But she didn't take the bait. Instead she pointed at the set of chairs on the other side of the pool. "There's plenty of space."

With a glance in the direction she was pointing, I let out a sigh and made my way over, my very hard tail between my legs.

8

CHELSEA

When I woke from my nap by the pool, Liam was gone, and despite my better judgment, my chest sank. We'd been hard-core flirting earlier, which wouldn't have been an entirely bad thing if it weren't for the fact that my tiny nugget of a crush was growing faster than I was ready for. I still didn't even know the guy, and even if I did, he wouldn't be staying long.

I wasn't surprised to find out that Liam was a former athlete. Something about the way he cut through the water looked like he'd been doing it his whole life. There were times I'd wondered if he ever came up for air, but I knew now he was just that well trained.

That was one mystery solved, but I had a strong feeling that Liam was hiding something bigger than an old career as a swimmer. And while I was curious to find out more about him, it was only fair for me to hide my writing from him. I had never shown my writing to anyone, let alone discussed the content. So far, Liam knew more than anyone else in my life, including Maisey.

Sure, my best friend knew I loved creative writing. We'd taken plenty of classes together in high school and college for her to know that much. But she didn't know that I'd been secretly writing novels and hiding them under my bed as if I would get in trouble for them.

Maisey and I were complete opposites. After obtaining her masters, Maisey had locked down a paralegal position at her father's law firm and had no plans of stopping soon. For her, there'd only been one man in her life. She'd been in love with Roger since we were freshmen in high school, even though they hadn't started dating until college. Basically, Maisey had her shit together, while I did not.

She was practical while I was whimsical, and I couldn't imagine her supporting my crazy new venture. I'd finally sent my book off to my chosen editor that morning and immediately started plotting another. I was going to see this dream through if it was the last thing I did, no matter my fears.

I showered off the sun from the day, washed my hair, and threw on a pair of panties and a black crop top sans the bra. Surprisingly, I'd gotten a lot of rewrites done. With Liam as my inspiration, the ideas flowed like an open faucet. I would reward myself tonight with a movie and chill.

When a knock came at the door, I froze in a panic. Tempted to ignore it completely, I threw on some boy shorts just in case I lost the courage. My heart raced, and I knew it was because I'd been trying to avoid thoughts of Liam. Why did he have to make it so impossible?

He'd been such a distraction at the pool, even sitting on the other side of it. With his bronze skin and sexy abs, and his navy trunks that were tight enough to announce his arousal every time I shifted my position. The only thing I found myself jotting in my idea book were notes about *him*. His tall and lean body, his cocky sense of humor, his alternative style.

By the end of the day, I'd had my next book, *Hero*, plotted with no effort at all.

I swung open my front door, expecting to see Liam's sideways grin and his goofy charm ready to encourage me to do something I knew I shouldn't do, like go to dinner or go for a naked swim in the pool—which, of course, I would turn down—but it wasn't Liam at all.

"Dean?" I felt my face drain of blood.

My ex-boyfriend looked amazing in a silver button-down shirt, black trousers, and his short natural waves perfectly combed back. When I'd been a little girl and had pictured my future husband, he had been the spitting image of Dean with his pretty green eyes, cleanly shaven face, broad shoulders, and friendly smile combined with his businesslike appearance. At first glance, he was utter perfection.

But then I remembered the frequent late nights at the accounting office where he interned and the brazen forgetfulness of my birthday and our two-year anniversary and the way he shamelessly flirted with his clients right in front of me at work functions, and my stomach churned with discomfort.

"Hey, beautiful. Aren't you going to invite me in?"

His easy smile, his confident greeting, it was like it had slipped his mind that we'd broken up two months ago. My blood started to boil.

What the hell? I let out a laugh to cover my growing anger. "That's probably not a good idea. I've already got plans."

Dean's eyes slipped not so subtly down my body and took in my attire. My I-definitely-do-not-have-plans attire, and his perfect smile grew wider. "I could join you, order us some takeout, hang out on the couch just like old times."

"More like ancient times. Dean, movie nights with you were torture. Your eyes were glued to your phone, and you always asked me to explain everything going on because you weren't paying attention."

Something flashed in his eyes, and his jaw hardened slightly. "Look, Chels, I miss you. I'm here to fix whatever the hell I did wrong to make you leave me." He reached inside his pocket and shoved his phone at me. "Here, hide it from me. I don't care. I just want to be with you again."

My heart should have melted like glaciers in the sun. This was what all women wanted, right? To be the one who got away? To have an ex realize just how much they were missing out on? I thought if it ever happened to me that I would feel conflicted, torn by my stubbornness to show him how well I was doing without him and my desire to have what we'd left behind. Except—I didn't have those feelings of regret. Not a shred, and it was the first time since our breakup that I realized it.

"I'm sorry, Dean. As I said, I already have plans. You should go." I started to close the door, but Dean's hand shot out, keeping it open.

"Wait." He spoke on a rushed breath. "Can't we just talk for a minute?" His gentle eyes were wide and filled with desperation. "When you broke up with me, I didn't think you really meant it, Chels. I thought you were just angry."

"I was angry." I laughed, still managing to keep my rising frustration at bay. "I was angry, and you didn't give a shit, so we broke up. It's actually very simple."

"But I love you. You can't just walk away from us like we never mattered."

"Really? Because I think she already did." The deep voice behind Dean shocked my heart right out of my chest.

Dean looked just as shocked when he jumped and spun around. "Whoa. Who the hell are you?"

Liam stepped around Dean and stood at my door, just in

front of me. "None of your business, mate, but you can call me Willy."

Liam turned to me and winked. My face flamed at our inside joke.

Dean did a double take between Liam and me, then his eyes stuck on the Hogues' houseguest, who was dressed in nothing but a pair of sweatpants that hung low on his hips. "Do you know this guy, Chels?"

It only took a second for me to figure out that Liam had given me the out that I needed to ensure Dean never came back. I stepped forward and wrapped my arms around Liam's waist, trying to ignore just how perfectly we fit.

"Actually, yes." I looked up at Liam with a syrupy smile. "*Willy* here is my date tonight." Even though I turned back toward Dean to speak, I could feel Liam's stare on me along with his arms gently tightening around me.

"That's right," Liam said as he leaned toward me.

Before I knew what was happening, Liam's lips were on my cheek, and they weren't quick to pull away. They lingered, giving Dean time to register everything happening. I didn't know if I ever would.

My cheeks burned, and I was thankful for the dark sky. "Dean, it was—um—nice of you to drop by."

Suddenly, I wasn't annoyed Dean had shown up fully expecting me to forgive him and move on with our relationship. Instead, I felt elated to have someone as an ally, no matter that I knew I should stay far away from that same man. Temporarily, Liam's company didn't feel like that bad of a thing.

Dean backed away, shaking his head with disgust. "Whatever, Chels. You're going to regret this."

Dean was long gone by the time I took my next breath then turned to Liam, who was still fully wrapped in my arms. I pulled away like his touch suddenly burned me. "Thanks for that."

Liam shrugged. "Figured the guy wasn't taking your rejection well. Poor bloke. I was on the back porch when I saw him pull up. I wasn't trying to pry. I promise, but I didn't know if someone was trying to break in through the back gate."

I laughed at that and stepped back into the pool house. "Well, I'm glad you're the new night watch. I guess that means I can enjoy my movie in peace." I smiled and put my hand on the doorknob. "Have a good night, Liam."

His brows rose. "Wait, that's it? I save your life again, and you shut the door on me? I thought we had a date tonight."

My cheeks were starting to hurt from smiling. "You want to come in and watch a movie with me? It will probably be a chick flick with a lot of cheesy writing. You don't strike me as a *Pretty Woman* kind of guy."

Liam gasped in mock offense. "You've got me all wrong, Chelsea Banks. I happen to love *Pretty Woman*, *The Notebook*, *Sleepless in Seattle*. Shall I continue?"

Laughing, I shook my head. "No, please. I get it. You're a regular romance addict." I stepped back to make room for him. "I'm about to make dinner and start the movie. Do you like wine?"

His smile widened, practically blinding me with its wattage. "I love the stuff."

It wasn't until after I shut the door and he was walking in front of me to the kitchenette that I recalled he was shirtless, his pants hanging so low that one slip would reveal the crack of his ass. I bit my lip to stop the urge to tell him to put a shirt on. The truth was, I didn't want him to put his shirt on. Maybe by the end of the night he would lose his sweatpants too.

9

LIAM

Chelsea poured us each a glass of Merlot and tossed a box of frozen pizza on the counter. I chuckled and looked at her curiously. "Pizza again?"

She shrugged, not at all ashamed. "That's what I was planning to have tonight. Take it or leave it."

"I'll take it. But just plain cheese? Where are all the toppings?"

"Ah." Chelsea held up her finger then walked back to the refrigerator.

She pulled out a bunch of ingredients and set them on the counter in front of me. Mozzarella cheese, tomatoes, and fresh basil.

"What's all this?"

"Pizza toppings. It's so good. Just wait."

And I did. I had zero issues with waiting and watching as Chelsea bustled around the kitchen, placing more ingredients on our pizza then sliding it into the oven. Never had someone so small looked so sexy executing such a simple task.

She was an effortless beauty with her red hair spun up in a messy bun, the sun from earlier in the day making her skin glow in the dim lighting. But my feelings were nothing new, and I wasn't just thinking about how tan her body had looked at the pool earlier in the day. My first impression of the fair-skinned seductress had been how strong and powerful she seemed.

I remembered the way she'd stuck up for herself with that woman at her parents' tearoom then again in our first encounter when she'd come out to tell me to turn down my music. It had manifested even in the way she'd wanted to refuse my help after getting stabbed by the cactus and now as she confidently set the oven timer and took a swig of her wine.

Chelsea wasn't just a stunning woman. She was beautifully intriguing and wholly unique. The best part was I knew I'd only just scraped the surface. Her eyes met mine as she brought down her wine glass.

"What?" She ran a finger below her lips. "Did I spill?"

I shook my head. "Nope. Just doing my research."

She squinted in confusion before widening her eyes and shaking her head with animated movement. "No. Uh-uh. You are not drawing my tattoo. I didn't agree to that."

"I am drawing something for you. Whether you use it or not is completely up to you."

She relaxed slightly and took another sip of wine before setting it on the counter and letting out a light laugh. "No offense. It's just—"

"Personal," I finished for her and watched closely as she nodded. "And you don't want to feel pressured to like whatever I create."

She nodded again.

"Lucky for you, I don't get easily offended."

"So, if I tell you I don't like your artwork you won't get

offended?" She pointed to my arms. "That would be equiva-
lent to me not liking your tattoos."

"You haven't even looked at my tattoos."

"I've seen them plenty, and I'm staring at them now,
aren't I?"

Chelsea was a cheeky one, with a sassy mouth, and I knew
just what to do with it. "Come closer."

Something deep in my gut told me she'd been waiting for
the invite ever since the day we'd met and her eyes had
tracked them like she would a suspect before the arrest. She
was curious, almost bashful. It made me eager to offer her a
chance to explore, to make her feel less guilty for wanting to
ask. Now, she didn't have to.

Without hesitation, she stalked forward, moved around the
island, and stood before me—mere inches from putting her
chest to mine. Then she explored. It started with her eyes,
perfect little orbs outlining each design like a critic at an art
museum. She was my critic now. With each second that
passed, as she studied me and I watched her, I claimed her
with every selfish bone in my body.

It took everything I had not to place my hands on that
small waist and pull her closer. To not lean into her scent and
inhale it like it was my only source of oxygen. I stayed put,
letting her eyes wander over my bare arms while I watched the
transparency on her face.

She wanted to ask questions. That was obvious by the way
her eyes would stop on one particular design. Her mouth
would open then shut really fast before she moved on to
another.

She wanted to touch my skin. Every now and then, her
hand would twitch, and instead of running her fingers up my
forearm, she would pull them back and run them through her
hair.

She wanted to lick me too. Okay, maybe that was just my interpretation of what was going on in Chelsea Banks's beautiful brain, but I would have encouraged her to lick me if that was what pleased her. It certainly would have pleased me.

"Fuck it." I said the words aloud, but I didn't think she heard. I placed my hands on her hips and pulled her forward just an inch. "Don't be shy, Chelsea Banks. Tell me what you think. Love 'em, hate 'em?"

She blew out a breath. It hit my shoulder and skated down my arm. "I don't hate any of it. It's all beautiful, Liam." She wasn't fucking with me. She wasn't trying to impress me. I'd gotten to know Chelsea enough to know her goal was never to bullshit.

"You're beautiful."

Her eyes snapped to mine, then she drew in a quick breath as her eyes slipped to my lips. *Fuck.* I wanted to take her right there, dart my tongue into her mouth and pick her up by her bum so I could fuck her into tomorrow like I'd been dreaming of doing since the second we met.

She was breathing so heavily, and I wondered how long it had been for her. When had she broken up with the bloke who'd just left her place after an all-too-desperate attempt to win her affection back?

Which brought me to another strong suit about Chelsea Banks. She didn't fuck around with men. When she was done, she was done, and no amount of groveling would win her back. I respected the fuck out of that. It also kind of shook me to my core. I wasn't sure why. Maybe it was because I wouldn't be there if it weren't for the fact that I'd broken three hearts on national television. Something told me that Chelsea would look at me a whole lot differently if she knew my true reasons for being here.

Her touch drew me from my thoughts. She was following

the outline of a tattoo on my left shoulder. "Can you tell me about this one?"

I looked down, but I already knew which one she was referencing. "That's the bridge my brother and I used to sword fight on when we were kids. That's his name spelled out with rocks from the creek. See it?"

"Yes," she whispered when her gaze fell on the shape of the letters.

I loved her reaction, how her pink lips parted slightly, and she sucked in another surprised breath.

"Are these swallows?"

She traced the birds that flew above the bridge, and I had to control my next breath. Chelsea wasn't the first woman to ever touch my tattoos. I loved it when women touched them, even the women who feigned interest as an excuse to touch me. But Chelsea was most definitely the first woman to peruse not just the designs but the intricacies of their lines and every shade of color. She was also questioning the meaning behind each design so intensely it was starting to make my chest rattle.

"They are," I answered, nearly forgetting the question. But at the sound of my raspy voice—a traitor to my emotions—I cleared my throat to try again. My hands were still on her waist as she touched me, and suddenly I wished I was wearing something other than sweatpants.

"The swallow that's flying apart from the flock, that's my brother, free from the grief that I held on to for way too long. And that one is me." I pointed to the bird behind him, leading the rest of the flock. "When I finally let him go and chose to celebrate his life rather than tarnish his memory with my own fuckups."

Her eyes flickered to mine then back down to a set of rings. "For your time in the Olympics."

I grinned. "The glory days."

"Why'd you quit?"

Swallowing, I debated what I should tell her and just how much. Then I realized it didn't really matter. Chelsea was safe. She was a stranger who I would know for a short time in my life then probably never see again. "For a while, I kept swimming for my brother, for his memory, in his honor. I beat the crap out of myself trying to outperform my own records, time and time again. Even my trainer tried to get me to slow down, but I couldn't. If I wasn't swimming, I was drowning in thoughts of Blake. I was pushing too hard, but even when my body started showing signs of wear and tear, I didn't quit. That led to one injury after another after another until I was cut from the team and forced to reevaluate my life."

"And did you?" She dropped her hands from my arm but didn't make a move to step away. "Did you reevaluate your life?"

I shrugged, something inside me hardening at the thought of telling her more. "Not right away, no. I became quite the fuckup actually. I went from star Olympic athlete to the man who lived in his parents' basement until his late twenties. I wasted a lot of years."

"You're not a fuckup." The seriousness in her tone caught me off guard. She had my full attention. "You went through something no one should ever have to go through, and you were handling it the best way you knew how. We're not supposed to have all our shit figured out, Liam. Anyone who pretends they do is lying. What matters is that you're here today and that you're doing good things with the time you're given." She inched forward, making my heart leap to life at her proximity. "So, what are you doing with your time, Liam Colborn?"

A flurry of emotions swirled in my chest, a complex

mixture of fear and hope and excitement. I wanted to kiss her. I wanted to push her away. I wanted to throw her onto the couch and fuck her into tomorrow. Why did Chelsea test me, and my thoughts, in a way I'd never let another get remotely close to? And why did it thrill me and terrify me in equal measure?

"I guess I'm figuring that out," I finally said, releasing my hands from her waist. My words were truer than she could understand, and our conversation only poured cold water on a moment that could have ended much differently.

As if she could read my thoughts, she took a step back then another, though a smile slowly appeared on her face. "Well, that makes two of us."

10

CHELSEA

We ate our pizza on opposite ends of the couch
while watching *Win a Date with Tad Hamilton!*—
his pick, not mine—laughing at all the ridiculous lines and putting some physical and emotional space
between us. After our conversation in the kitchen earlier, I felt
like we both needed it.

It was strange, but I got the feeling that Liam could use a
friend right then, attraction aside. It was nice to have him
around to break up what could be a mundane week just brain-
storming ideas for my next book and watering succulents. He
was funny and nice to look at, and clearly I needed someone
around to save me from myself on the regular. Not only that,
but I felt stimulated just from his presence, like being around
him made me feel more comfortable in my own skin. He
made me feel bold, confident, safe. Probably because I knew
he would be gone soon, back to London and to whatever life
he'd needed to get away from.

I got up to pour myself another glass of wine and brought
the bottle over to refill his too. He looked up, green eyes

sparkling with fresh amusement from my favorite scene in the movie. Tad had just showed up at the Piggly Wiggly to ask the heroine on the date.

"Thanks, love."

I would never get over Liam's accent or the way my insides tingled as he spoke. He could literally say anything, and my body would quiver. I smiled and sat on the middle cushion before tucking my legs under me.

"We should venture out tomorrow. Maybe go downtown again and check out the parks."

My gaze slid to his. By the flickering light of the television, I could see his eyes already locked on me. "Sure. But I need to work at some point."

"Bring your work, and I'll bring mine."

I didn't exactly know what Liam's work consisted of since he was supposedly between contracts. "So, I'll bring my note-book, and you'll bring your…" I trailed off, waiting for him to fill in the blank.

He smiled and turned back to the television. "I'll bring my notebook too."

Laughing, I shook my head and turned back to the screen, trying to let the movie replace every thought of the very sexy, and still shirtless, man sitting next to me. It was an impossible task, but I definitely earned an E for effort by the time the credits started rolling.

Our wine was gone. The room was still dark, and the soundtrack to the movie played on as neither of us moved. It was late. Without a clock in sight, my guess was that it was nearing midnight, and if I wanted to have a clear head tomor-row, I would need to head to bed.

"I should bog off." Liam shifted.

My mood dimmed, and my heart squeezed while my mind screamed for him to stay. What was wrong with me? Liam was like one giant red flag that waved boldly and brightly, and I couldn't seem to heed the warning. I didn't want him to *bog off*.

Then he stood, making my chest ache even more. He held out his hands, and I took them, letting him help me to my feet and wrap me straight in his arms. He held me firmly, applying pressure just slightly as I slid my arms around him and squeezed him back.

Damn, he even hugged like a pro. If embracing was an Olympic sport, I was certain he would earn all the gold medals.

"Thanks for rescuing me, once again." My cheek was flat against his chest as I spoke. I sensed his smile in return.

"You didn't need any rescuing tonight, but it was my pleasure to help you chase that bloke away. I'll be your Willy anytime you need one, love."

We chuckled, but I could feel my body heat at the innuendo behind his words. I wondered how true that was. There was clearly something between us, chemistry I hadn't felt in a very long time. But the disappointment that came with even humoring that idea was a heavy blow.

I lifted my cheek to face him and smiled. "Good to know."

His stare grew more intense with my words, like maybe he was hoping for an invite. How I managed to hold his gaze with my heart racing in my chest was a mystery all on its own.

Then his eyes darted between mine. He leaned down, soft lips brushing my cheek just slow enough to send a wave of chills blasting through my body. I didn't mean to hold him tighter, but it was either that or melt into a puddle at his feet.

When his mouth hit my ear, my lids slammed closed, and I sucked in a sharp breath. My skin tingled everywhere. My heart galloped, and when I felt Liam grow hard beneath his sweatpants, I knew I wasn't imagining a single thing.

"You are quite lovely, Chelsea Banks."

He kissed my ear, so softly enough I thought I might have imagined it, then he kissed my cheek while running gentle circles on my back with his palm. God, he smelled good, like fresh basil and strong wine. If I played my cards right, he could be my second dinner—and maybe even my breakfast.

"You're not so bad yourself." I pulled in a steadier breath than the one before it and dared a look. Our mouths were only inches apart, and his hold on me indicated he had no intention of letting go. I slid my hand around from his back to his stomach then moved it up to his chest, savoring the deep valleys and perfect ridges of his muscles. Dean hadn't felt like that, like he was sculpted from God's best tools.

I'd been so focused on the feel of Liam that I'd almost missed that his hands had been roaming too. One was cupping my neck while the other had slipped beneath my shirt and now rested at my waist. He leaned in, breathing me in as he did. "I should go before you hate me in the morning."

I smiled, knowing exactly what he meant. We could let whatever this was between us get out of control. We could kiss. We could strip. We could make magic with our bodies. But then what? What would come from a night of unadulterated bliss? I wasn't ready to find out.

"Okay," I finally said, breathing the word on a whisper.

That broke the spell.

Liam took a step back, and I walked him to the door. He wrapped me in his arms for another hug before kissing my forehead then walking across the pool patio, out the gate, and out of sight.

I debated taking a cold shower, anything to settle my racing heart. I felt like I was back in grade school, locked in a coat closet with my biggest crush. I didn't know how to handle myself, what to say or do. While I felt more confident than I had in my life, I was also more nervous than I'd ever been before—and now frustrated.

With a groan, I kicked open my bedroom door and tore off my clothes. I didn't even bother to dress before slipping into bed and throwing my hands over my eyes. All I could see was Liam. His smile, those rock-hard abs. I could feel him too. Hard for me while all I wanted to do was melt for him.

When I adjusted slightly, the fabric of the sheet rubbed my hard nipple, making me shake with want. Would it have been so bad to pull Liam into my bedroom and fuck his brains out? We were both grown adults. Maybe holding back our attraction wasn't the right answer. Maybe we needed to give into it.

I moved, feeling the sheet rub against my nipples again. I shuddered. It had been a long time since anyone had touched me there. I ran a finger over them, imagining Liam using his hot, wine-flavored tongue on me, licking, sucking, savoring. He seemed like someone who would take his time, knowing just what to do to get me off, maybe even more than once. But more than I craved his touch, I wanted to feel him inside me.

My fingers moved between my legs and slid through my wet center. He hadn't even touched me. Hadn't even kissed me, and I was nearly there. I couldn't go through the night without getting myself off.

A vision from earlier that morning flashed through my mind. I'd gone to the Hogues' to drop off the mail, and I'd heard noises coming from the basement. Part of me had known that Liam was down there, that I shouldn't step a foot closer, but my curiosity got the better of me. When I saw the door to his room open, I knew I shouldn't have taken that peek inside. It was wrong on so many levels, but the fact that I'd stayed to watch him pleasure himself was far worse than any sin I'd ever committed.

I placed two fingers on my clit and rubbed while replaying

my visit to Liam's room, where I'd peered through the crack of the already opened door and had to brace myself at the sight.

He'd kicked the blue sheets of his bed down around his feet, his underwear tossed beside the bed. His knees had been up, and his hand had gripped his veiny cock, moving up and down with a rhythm that told me he'd done it a million times before. His abs had tightened and his breathing had intensified. I had wanted him to be thinking about me.

As much as I'd wanted to watch him finish himself off, my morals had finally kicked in. It had been wrong to look in the first place, but now, it was all that played in my mind while I slid two fingers deep inside myself and worked myself to the brink.

My right hand moved to my heaving breasts and squeezed while I quickened my movements with my other hand, which had just struck gold. With Liam on my mind, our hug from tonight in my heart, and my fingers in my pussy, stars burst beneath my squeezed eyelids. I came alive.

11

W hen I knocked on Chelsea's door in the morning, she was all ready to go. She stepped out and turned to lock her door. *Damn*, was my first thought.

She was dressed in white jean shorts that showed off her perfect sun-kissed legs, a pale-blue T-shirt that was tucked into her shorts, and tan sandals. Her hair was down and lightly curled around her shoulders, and the only touch of makeup she appeared to be wearing was a layer of gloss on her lips.

She carried a small backpack that she threw over her shoulders then smiled. "Ready to go?"

"Hey. That was my line."

Chelsea stepped forward with a little laugh, placing her sunglasses over her eyes and walking past me toward the gate. "It's mine now."

That exchange was my first clue as to how the day would go. Flirtation. It was right where we'd left off last night, and right where we would pick up that day.

"How'd you sleep?" I asked once she was buckled in the driver's seat.

I swore her cheeks darkened a shade. "Fine. And you?"

I studied her face a little longer, confirming a blush was creeping up her cheeks. It could have meant anything, but I wanted to imagine Chelsea getting naughty after I left last night. I sure as hell had. After all the sexual tension that had been suffocating us during our drawn-out goodbye, I couldn't have gone to sleep without a little release. Chelsea had no idea the effect she'd had on me since I'd met her.

My lips twitched with amusement. "I was pretty wound up, so I worked out a little, then I slept like a baby."

If she had turned to look at me, she would have seen the sly smile on my face, a tell that my workout consisted of one hand and thoughts of the bombshell in the driver's seat. But she didn't turn, so my secret was mine to keep.

She drove us to the same area we'd parked the other day for lunch, then we crossed the street to the entrance to Water-place Park. We walked along the river and then across it, finally settling under a tree where she pulled out a blanket and laid it down for us to sit on.

"Another beautiful day in Providence. We never luck out with weather like this back home."

"Really?"

"Not for this many days in a row. Have you ever been? To London?"

She shook her head. "I've never left this area." Then she smiled at me sheepishly. "Sad, I know, but I've never had a reason to go."

"You don't need a reason to travel other than to want to experience life. C'mon, Chelsea. You're a writer. You can't possibly tell me you're not curious about the places you write about."

She laughed. "Sure, but there's this thing called the internet. I can look up pretty much anything, and that's just as good."

I could feel my eyes bulging in my head. "I can't believe I just heard that. You're honestly telling me that you're not learning anything more right now by sitting under this tree than you would watching a streaming video site?"

Chelsea shrugged, and her smile faded. "Sometimes that's as good as it's going to get, and some of us have to be okay with that. My parents traveled plenty, but they never once took me on vacation. I paid for college on my own, which meant I didn't have a single dime to spare."

"Wait a second. Your parents didn't help you with college?"

She shook her head, seeming confused by my surprise. "My parents are comfortable and happy, but they don't make a lot of money. Besides, a lot of my peers had to pay their own way. That's what loans are for."

"But you dropped out of school?"

"It's complicated."

I folded my arms across my chest and grinned. "I've got time."

Smiling, she shook her head and started to tell me the short version of her college story. "I got a late start at school. After high school, I didn't have any desire to go to college, so I took up odd jobs just to afford a small room in a house I shared with three other girls. After a couple of years, I felt unsettled and kind of guilty for not going to school like my parents had always encouraged me to, so I got my associate degree at a community college then moved on to a four-year college to get my bachelor's in communications. When I still hadn't decided what to do with my degree, I continued on to get my master's in business. I took up nannying full-time to pay for what I could, so it was taking me forever to earn my credits. Eventually, I realized that I would rather nanny than go to school. Thirty credits shy of graduating."

She laughed, but I couldn't find the humor in what she was telling me. I always wished I had pursued higher education in something, everything. And there she was with nearly three college degrees she'd paid for and earned on her own. No matter what she wound up doing, she would always have her education.

She sighed. "Anyway, two months ago, I dropped out."

"To write?"

She nodded, holding her notebook tighter to her chest.

"Can I read something?"

She looked down at my sketchbook. "Only if I can look at what you've drawn."

I grinned, ready to accept her challenge with a little twist of my own. "I have a better idea." Then I stood, dusted off my khaki shorts, and pointed to the tree across from her on the other side of the trail. "I'm going to sit over there and sketch. You'll be here writing. When we're done, we'll show each other what we worked on."

For a second, she just looked at me like she didn't know whether I was bluffing or not. Maybe she was scared to actually go through with it and show me something she pulled from that beautiful brain of hers and put onto paper. Eventually she nodded and mumbled something like "Okay."

My tree was not nearly as comfortable as the one she'd chosen. Hers seemed perfect for lounging, while mine had roots growing all over the place above ground. Eventually, I nestled into a spot, which I made a home of for the next few hours as we worked in silence. Every now and then, I would look up and catch her staring off into space. She was beautiful in those quiet moments, and with each glance, I grew more eager to look at what she was scribbling in that tiny blue note-book. Every so often, she would catch my sneaky glances with one of her own, and her cheeks would blush in response.

I must have checked the time over a dozen different instances, hoping for the excuse to break for lunch so we could meet up again. She was the one to make the first move. After shoving her blue notebook in her bag and standing up, she walked halfway toward me, and I met her in the middle. I offered her my sketchbook so she could look at what I'd drawn.

She shook her head. "I need a drink first. Lunch?"

I chuckled and gestured for her to lead the way. This time she chose the restaurant, which was fine by me. Chelsea took me to a small deli with outside seating where she ordered us a bottle of white wine to share. I happily obliged, getting the sense that Chelsea's nerves were getting the better of her at the idea of me reading her work. After she downed her first glass, she handed her notebook to me.

"Let's get this over with. Me first."

Her notebook had a silky bookmark running through its pages, so I turned to the page marked and started reading. The description of the male sounded a lot like me, the way she described his hair, his body, and his British accent. I laughed as I realized she had written about the night she'd found me swimming in the Hogues' pool with the music too loud, and now it was me blushing profusely at the way she described the water dripping down my torso, over peaks and valleys of terrain that had her pulse quickening.

I read the pages a few times before finally handing the notebook back to her and popping a smile on the side of my mouth. "Your words are lovely—quite poetic, in fact. Is your book about me?"

She let out a laugh. "Are you offended? I was struggling to

find inspiration for my male hero, and you happened to come along at the right time."

"I'm no woman's hero, love. But I'm flattered, not offended."

She shrugged. "It's fiction. Don't get too cocky about it."

Then we both smiled, and I could feel us sharing a mutual moment.

"Okay," she finally said, reaching out to me. "Hand it over. I showed you mine. Now you show me yours."

I cocked an eyebrow, my resolve to stay friendly with this girl dissolving faster than sugar in water. She was a little temptress, and she didn't even know it. I slid my sketchbook over to her, my heart suddenly ricocheting in my chest. Nerves weren't something I felt often. I'd been drawing my entire life. It wasn't something I hid or felt shy about, but with Chelsea as my subject, I couldn't help feeling nervous about whether she would like my work or not.

The moment Chelsea opened the sketchbook and her eyes fell on what I'd been working on beneath the tree, her eyes widened then zoomed into the image like lasers. It was almost exactly the way she'd looked at my tattoos last night except, this time, her eyes started to redden and water.

"Is this for me?"

It wasn't hard to guess her question. The sketch centered around a typewriter with a section of paper coming out from the top. A shaded heart marked the center of the paper.

"It is, but it's only my first attempt. If you don't like it—"

"I love it," she jumped in, her eyes moving from mine back down to the sketch. "I love it so much." Then her eyes gleamed as they met mine again. "I learned how to write on a typewriter."

"I didn't know that."

She shook her head. "I know, but this—resonates. I love it, Liam, a lot."

"And the shaded heart represents what you write. Romance in all its forms is what you told me—messy, real, all its shades."

She smiled even bigger and nodded. "Liam, this is—" She met my eyes one last time. "Perfect."

"Then let's get it put on you."

Chelsea let out a laugh. "What? Now?"

I laughed, too, loving her reaction because somewhere in there was excitement over the thrilling thought of inking up her body. "Well, after lunch. Let's eat, then I want to take you somewhere."

She sucked in a deep breath, waited a few seconds, then nodded. "Okay."

12

CHELSEA

After lunch, Liam used the GPS on his phone to navigate us south a few blocks and around the corner to a tattoo shop, where I immediately halted in my tracks.

He grabbed my hand and squeezed. "Trust me, Chelsea."

That was all I needed to hear to unclench my body and follow him into the building. The AC blasted my nerves like a hit of adrenaline, and I sighed, releasing my built-up tension.

Is this really about to happen? I've gone my entire adult life without committing to branding my body. Am I really going to let it happen now? Just because a cute Brit decided to draw me something that actually feels perfect? It could just be the crush I have on him, or the fact that I had two glasses of wine at lunch.

Liam didn't let go of my hand when the door to the shop shut behind us or even when he stepped forward to talk to the burly bearded man with ink covering every inch of his body.

"Hiya, my friend here is looking into getting her first tattoo. I wondered if you'd perhaps be able to do a temporary on her. She could wear it around and see if it's something she wants to keep."

The burly man looked me over beneath bent brows like he was assessing my naked skin, wondering if I was worth his time. "Sure, whatever," he finally said with a shrug. "If you want to choose a design, I can make a temp."

Liam set his sketchbook on the table and pointed at the drawing he'd made for me. "Actually, can you do something custom?"

The man shrugged. "Sure, whatever." Then he slid Liam a piece of paper. "Draw it on this transfer, and we'll be good to go."

Liam let go of my hand to take the sheet from the man and we sat on a couch in the back corner of the room. As he drew the sketch again, I couldn't help but watch the way he bent his brows together and bit his bottom lip in concentration. It was almost as sexy as the art he'd made just for me.

A chill rushed through me. I'd been thinking about getting a tattoo for years, but I hadn't once stepped inside a tattoo parlor, let alone come close to committing to the type of ink I would want permanently placed on my body. It was crazy to think Liam would be the artist of something that I would keep forever. Was it too much? Was I overthinking? I was certain the answer was yes to both questions, but at that moment, I didn't care.

He finished with a little smile and a glance up at me. "It's just a temp, Chelsea. Relax. No commitments. Not yet anyway." He winked, and I swore a flock of butterflies took flight in my chest.

Why did he have to be so adorably—British? He was supposed to be the annoyingly arrogant houseguest that I wouldn't even remember once he left. And now… I swallowed and let out a laugh. "I'm excited, I promise. I've just never come this close to getting a tattoo before."

"Well, now you can be certain that you want one permanently first." With that, he stood and held out his hand, which I took without blinking. It felt natural, my hand in his, and when I got up to meet him, my hand fell to his chest. "Wait. I don't know where I want to put it."

Liam moved the hair over my shoulder and touched my back between my shoulder blades. "How about here?"

Chills swept over my body, and I almost burst out my agreement before thinking about it. "I don't know. Then I'll never be able to see it."

He swept my hair again, this time moving it back over my shoulders, and pointed to a spot above my chest without touching it. "Maybe here?"

I shook my head. "No, I don't like that."

"Here?" He swept his fingers over the top of my arm, and I shook my head again.

Liam took the sketch and held it over my waist. "What if you put it here? Just below your bikini line?"

I swallowed and looked down at where he was placing the transfer, then I nodded slowly at the idea of that one. "Yes. Maybe there."

He smiled and pulled me toward the burly dude with the long beard and museum of tattoos covering his body. "Let's see how it looks on her bikini line." Then he turned to me. "Left side?"

I nodded.

The man grunted something and stood from his desk before waving for me to follow him through a doorway that led to a row of rooms. Liam stayed close behind. I was glad I didn't have to ask him to, but I didn't think he would let me out of his sight even if I wanted him to.

We entered a room with a chair that reminded me of what I sat in at my dentist's office. On the table beside the man's stool sat an array of tools and cleaning equipment with stacks of drawers beneath it. While everything looked perfectly clean and organized, I felt like I was getting in way over my head.

I turned back to Liam and shook my head. "This is crazy," I hissed. Surely, the man behind me could hear me, so I wasn't sure why I whispered.

Liam chuckled and placed his hand on my stomach. "It's just a temporary tattoo. You never have to come back here if you don't like it." Then he gently applied pressure, enough to push me back into the chair.

I stared up at him, my mouth falling open, ready to tell him off, when the burly man behind me growled, *actually* growled.

"Are we doing this or what? I have an appointment in three minutes."

I sucked in a deep breath, narrowed my eyes at Liam to let him know he was in deep shit when this was over, then leaned back in the chair. "Fine. Let's get this over with."

"You're going to need to pull down your pants, sweetheart."

Out of my peripheral, I caught Liam's smirk, which only made me want to kick him out of the room, but there was no way in hell I was letting him leave. So instead of fighting this one, I unbuttoned my jean shorts and pulled them down, along with my underwear, as low as possible without introducing the two men to my lady bits.

In less than a minute, Liam's art was on my pelvis, centered at my bikini line, and the tattoo artist handed me a mirror so I could see it better.

"What do you think?"

I grinned up at him, instantly forgiving him for pushing me into the chair before I was ready. "I think I'm in love."

Liam's grin grew wider as his eyes traveled down to where I was nearly exposed. "I think I am too."

I released my shorts with my left hand so I could swat him with it, then I smiled up at the tattoo artist, who was already rising from his chair. "Thank you for this. Do I make an appointment if I decide to get the real thing?"

"Or just swing by. Someone here will be able to do it. It's small enough. Shouldn't take too long."

The second we stepped out of the tattoo parlor, I grabbed Liam's arm and laughed. "It almost feels like I got the real thing." Then I looked up at him with an amused glare. "I can't believe you pushed me into that chair."

"Oh, stop," he said with a roll of his eyes. "I barely touched you, but you sure pulled those knickers down in a jiffy."

I went to swat him again, but his hand caught mine, and he threaded his fingers through mine. "Now it's my turn. Take me somewhere. Impress me with your Providence knowledge."

It wasn't too hard to think of where to take Liam next. The man loved art, and Providence had plenty of that to offer. I took him on a walking tour of everything I knew, including huge metal sculptures and wall canvases nearby.

Finally, I took him back through Waterplace Park, where we took our time strolling over Venice-inspired bridges, admiring the street-vendor art, stopping to listen to music on the live stage, and taking a narrated boat tour down the river.

When it started to get dark, we grabbed dinner at an outdoor café then moved to the bar to drink more wine. I hadn't even noticed how many hours had passed or that we'd stayed in the same four-mile radius all day long. Liam had a genuine interest in all that Providence had to offer, and I loved that I could be the one to show him around.

I laughed as he recounted my reaction at the tattoo parlor. "I've never seen someone so frightened to get a temporary tattoo before."

I placed a hand over my face. Now that I had more drinks in me, I was feeling ridiculous for how I'd acted earlier in the day. "It wasn't about the temporary tattoo," I said in an attempt to defend myself. "It was the first step to getting the real thing. Do you know how intimidating that place was to someone who's never even stepped in one before?"

Liam tilted his head and narrowed his eyes. "That was your first time? Really?"

I was grateful for the darkening sky so Liam couldn't see my blush. "It was. Between the drilling noises and Hagrid himself putting his hands on my lady bits, I don't know how I feel about getting a real one."

Liam's eyes sparkled as he leaned forward. "Between you and me, I'm not fond of Hagrid coming close to your lady bits either."

I leaned in, mimicking him. "And why are you so protective of my lady bits, Liam Colborn?"

He grinned then leaned in farther until his mouth touched my ear. I sucked in a breath to steady my heart as it leaped to life.

"Perhaps I'm just jealous the chump got closer than I have."

Chills whooshed over my body at his words. I tilted my mouth to his ear. "He's not here right now, is he?" I swallowed, shocked by my burst of confidence. "It's all about your perspective."

I pulled back slowly, almost expecting to see Liam wearing a shocked and appalled expression, but that wasn't what I found at all. His gaze slipped to my lips then locked on my eyes with an expression so intense it completely stole my breath. "I think my perspective is pretty perfect, actually."

My whole body seemed to come alive in that moment. We were so close, and I wanted nothing more than to lean in and close the gap between us.

"Can I get you two anything else?"

The voice of our server was like a splash of cold water. We pulled apart, my heart still speeding in my chest, then we let out simultaneous laughs.

"I think we're good," I told the man with a smile.

"Are you sure?" Liam asked, finishing the rest of his wine.

I nodded and reached for my wallet. "I want to show you one last thing before we head back."

He touched my hand that had grabbed my wallet and shook his head. "I've got this." Before I could argue, he was handing cash to our server and helping me up. "Lead the way, love."

From there, it was a short distance back to the riverwalk, where we made our way to one of the arched bridges. The air smelled of a campfire, and smoke swirled about the air, all while an eclectic soundtrack played over the crackling of wood and the chatter of the crowd. It was completely dark out, save for the firelight on the water, which had stolen Liam's attention.

"What is this?"

I smiled and pulled him to an open spot at the balcony. "WaterFire. Isn't it beautiful?"

Liam nodded, completely transfixed, staring out at the water where a riverboat that carried passengers passed one of the fire pits in the middle of the river. The fire had already been lit, and a man in the boat leaned over the fire to add wood to it.

"How many fires do you think there are?" His gaze traveled down the river to each of the fire pits.

"I think I read somewhere that there are over one hundred."

"This is incredible."

I nodded. Living in Providence, I could easily take this stuff for granted and forget it was there. "I guess you'd call it a spiritual communal ritual. It was created in the midnineties as a symbol of Providence's renaissance." I didn't pretend to know more than what I'd heard over the years, and Liam didn't question the art of it all. He simply leaned into the night show and watched as the soundtrack changed and more boats traveled by.

The crowds thickened, packing in around us, and Liam gave up his spot at the balcony for a family and stood behind me. Somehow, above all the senses that WaterFire captured, all I could see, hear, smell, or feel was Liam. He wrapped his arms around my middle and pressed his lips to my cheek, causing me to smile and sneak a peek at him over my shoulder.

He wore that intense gaze again. The one that, back at the café, told me we were on the verge of kissing. But this time, when I started to close the distance, he closed it first.

13

She tasted like campfire and wine—smoky, hot, and completely capable of making me drunk after one taste.

I grazed her bottom lip with my teeth, my head spinning with visions of Chelsea wrapping those same lips around other parts of me, especially the part of me that was twitching below my belt. It was no longer possible to be cautious with my thoughts or hands or mouth—to save her any more than I ought to save myself from a fling that could only end in disaster. All I wanted was this moment and the next, all *with* her, all *of* her. What would happen in two weeks or a month didn't matter. What she still didn't know about me could wait. Nothing mattered except for this kiss that sparked the air like the flames that licked the river water below us.

With my hands on her waist, I spun her body to face me, then I palmed the back of her neck, pulling her deeper into a kiss that I never wanted to end. She clung to me, her fingers gripping my sides like she needed the leverage to keep herself upright. When her tongue darted out, slipping between my lips and touching mine, I groaned and grew harder between her legs.

I pulled away, sucking in a breath and searching her eyes. They were glazed over, her mouth parted, and even under the night sky, I could see pink staining her cheeks. She was glowing, beautiful, and I knew I wouldn't be able to stand in that park another minute without ripping off her clothes.

"Want to get out of here?"

She nodded quickly, and I smiled before pulling her from the balcony to the riverwalk, where we rushed back to the car. Once we were inside, I leaned over the console, stealing another kiss as she tried to start her car. I placed my hand between her thighs and squeezed her bare leg, growling when I realized it would be at least another ten minutes before I could take off every scrap of fabric that kept us apart.

She let out a light laugh, this time successfully starting the car. I threw myself back into my seat, groaning at the erection still fighting my pants.

When we got on the road, I calmed down a little, enough to switch on the music to distract me from the sexy woman behind the wheel. I couldn't remember the last time I'd been so turned on, so desperate to get a woman naked. On *British Bachelor*, I'd made out with plenty of the women, nearly all of them, in fact. But I'd only gotten close to sleeping with two of them. In the end, I'd slept with none of them, something the viewers would never in a million years believe.

Every single viewer who commented on my social media accounts before I shut them down had something to say about "guys like me" who just went on the show to "get Insta-famous" and "rich." None of those comments applied to me, but no one would look deep enough to know the truth. Instead, the women from the show had become victimized heroes who should have won medals for putting up with a scam artist like me. And that just touched the surface of how I had been labeled after the final taping aired.

Before the show, I'd slept with women, but I couldn't remember it ever feeling like this.

Chelsea parked her car in front of the garage beside the entrance to the pool house then turned to me. "This is crazy, right? We've known each other for four days."

I reached out to take her hand, reveling at how small and dainty it was in mine. "You're overthinking it. Let's go inside, pour some wine, put on some music." The corner of my mouth tipped up in a smile. "And then…" I leaned over, brushing my lips against hers. "I'll let you touch my giant willy."

The sound of her laughter made me smile. This was how it should be—natural, easy, completely right.

"It's no joke, love. Just think, you'll have something to talk to Gwen about the next time you stop by the tearoom."

She laughed again, swatting me with her hand. I caught it and dragged it down my chest and onto the fabric of my trousers. As I stared deeply into her wide silver-moon eyes, I cupped her hand around the subject in question. While the size of any man's willy, big or small, was in the eye of the beholder, I was confident enough to know Chelsea wouldn't be disappointed. When her small hand squeezed, I kissed her firmly and breathed her in.

"Come with me," I whispered when I finally pulled away.

I made the first move to exit the car and took her hand when she approached. We passed through the main gate then through the pool gate and went straight to her pool house.

After entering, I shut the door and locked it behind me before leaning against it and letting out a breath. "C'mere."

Chelsea stepped up to me, the top of her head just reaching the top of my chest. I tilted her chin up, gripped her waist, and pulled her flush to my body. Slipping a hand beneath her blouse, I ran a finger against her silky-smooth skin, growing harder at the touch.

"I've never done this before."

Her quiet words made me freeze because I didn't understand what she meant. "Done what, love?"

Her breath shook as she exhaled. "I mean, I've only slept with guys who I've dated—not strangers. I've never had a one-night stand."

I shook my head, her words rattling me more than I knew they should. "We haven't known each other long, but I'm certainly not a stranger. And who said anything about this being a one-night stand? I'm happy to fuck you for as many days and nights as you wish."

My comment brought a smile to her lips, but it faded as her gaze filled with doubt.

"Chelsea." I tipped her chin up again. "I'd very much like to take you to bed but only if you want me to."

"I do."

Her quick answer gave me a burst of confidence, and I couldn't hold back my smile. "Well, then—"

"I just don't want to find out you're a psycho or anything." She blushed at her comment then shook her head like she was embarrassed. "I mean, I know you're not a psycho. But you haven't even told me why you left London so abruptly. Was it a girl? An ex? Is *she* a psycho?" Her eyes widened as if she'd just hit the jackpot. "You're married, aren't you?"

I laughed at the sudden random fire. "I'm not married, and there are no psychos on the loose. That I know of."

"Then what is it, Liam? What aren't you telling me?" She searched my eyes like she was desperately trying to find something wrong with the situation.

The more she questioned it, the more I did too. I didn't

want to risk something good ending, all because of the show and the media's twisted truths.

"Why are you staying at the Hogues' when they aren't even here?"

I tried my hardest to let her questions roll off my back, to keep things light and playful, but the truth was each question was just another brick in the wall being built between us. Her concerns were fair, but the fact that she was having any was the exact reason I needed to end whatever infatuation existed between us before things got too heavy. Chelsea had a life in Providence. My life, while messy and complicated and very public, was back in London. She deserved better than to get dragged into the mud of my life, especially when she was just getting started figuring out her own.

When I didn't answer her after a few moments, she took a step back and sighed. "Tonight was a mistake."

Her words stung more than anything a bunch of reality-television fans could ever say, but I also knew my place in this mess. I couldn't answer her questions. Therefore, I knew I deserved whatever punches she threw at me. "Yeah." I ran a hand through my hair. "Maybe you're right."

I thought I saw her bottom lip quiver, but it was over so fast I might have imagined it. She gestured to the door at my back and raised her brows. "You should probably go."

I swallowed, taking a moment to sort through my thoughts. I had to find a better way to handle the situation, but I didn't have time to think it through. Instead, I stood upright, turned, and left through the same door I'd entered from with Chelsea. This time, she slammed the door behind me.

14

Yesterday was the most productive writing day of my entire week. I locked myself in my house, turned on some ambient noise, and typed like I was trying to save my life. Not a single distraction came between me and my writing. Every so often, Liam would sneak into my mind, and I would shove him right back out, replacing him with the character version of him in my book.

I finally left my house the next day to get some fresh air and exercise, entering Spill the Tea a little past nine in the morning. My dad wiped down a table near the entrance while my mom stood near the front counter switching on the televisions.

"Hey, Dad." I greeted him with a hug.

He was a stout man, a former pro wrestler, who made up for his height with his build, and he gave the best hugs ever. My entire body warmed from his embrace, and I let out a smile when we parted.

"Hey, Bug." My dad had nicknamed me Bug when I was a curious little girl who was always digging around in our backyard, collecting insects, chasing fireflies, and searching for worms. "How's your week off?"

I shrugged, taking a seat at the table he was cleaning. "Not as relaxing as I thought it would be. It's funny, but I was almost more productive when I was trying to juggle my time between nannying and school." I left out the writing part and immediately felt a pit in my stomach for what I'd been keeping from my parents. "Dad—" I started, but we were interrupted by my mom, who came up to join us.

"Hey, sweetie. What brings you by so early?"

I looked between them, knowing I had a reason for my impromptu visit that my subconscious was clearly responsible for. "I need to talk to you two about something."

My mom registered my serious tone and sat beside my dad, a worried look on her face. "Is everything okay?"

I nodded. "Better than okay, actually. I just—well, this is hard because I know how much you two have supported my education and have encouraged me to get my doctorate, and I'm so grateful for all of it. But business school just isn't for me." I darted a glance between them. "I quit my internship two months ago, and I dropped out of college."

"You what?" my mom shrieked.

My dad rested a hand on her leg and leaned toward me. "Chelsea, that's quite the news. What on earth were you thinking?"

I sucked in a deep breath and released it slowly. "I was thinking that I was spending all this time putting hours into a career that I knew I wouldn't enjoy. I want to write books. I want to spend my days exploring all the stories that have been building inside me."

"Honey," my mom admonished. "You're almost thirty years old. You know we've been patient with your pacing in school, but to just quit and throw away years and years of college? I'm sorry, but I don't understand why you couldn't have completed your master's program. You were so close."

I'd anticipated this reaction, but that didn't make the conversation easier. "I will finish school one day. I promise those credits won't go to waste. But a master's in business is the wrong direction for me. While I figure out the right direction, I want to nanny, and I want to write."

"I think that's fair."

My head snapped in my dad's direction. "What?"

He shrugged, focusing on me and ignoring the panicked glare from my mom. "I think it's your life, Chelsea, and we will always support you in whatever you choose. Perhaps we pressured you into choosing a field that didn't suit you, and for that I'm sorry. I think you should give this writing thing a shot."

My mom did a double take between us. "Jeffrey, you cannot be serious right now."

He sighed and leaned over to take my hand in his. "Can we make a deal?"

I nodded, slightly hesitant since I didn't know what terms he was about to propose, but his reaction was more than I'd hoped for already. I would try to meet him somewhere in the middle.

"At some point in the next five years, you'll go back to school for whatever it is you want to pursue, and you'll finish your doctorate. It would be such a waste if you let all that time go."

I nodded, unable to hold back my giant grin. "You have my word that I'll go back. Perhaps for creative writing or a literature degree. I'm sorry I didn't tell you two sooner." This time I focused on my mom, who still seemed to be managing her shock. "I want you to be proud of me, but I also need to be happy and proud of myself. I needed to take this leap."

Just then, the sound of a familiar voice caught my attention. My pulse spiked, and my heart crashed like cymbals in my chest as I turned to search for Liam. His voice sounded like it was coming from somewhere in the tearoom. I hadn't seen him enter, but I knew without a doubt that it was him I was hearing. It was the same voice that had haunted my sleep, the voice that had crushed me when he'd agreed with me that our kiss had been a mistake.

After a full sweep of the room, I confirmed that no one had entered. Then my eyes caught on the image playing on one of the small televisions in the corner of the room, and every bone in my body chilled.

A man who very clearly looked like the Hogues' house-guest escorted a woman into a fancy restaurant. At least that was how it appeared. She was drop-dead gorgeous, blond, and wearing a stunning yellow evening gown. It was as if their outfits were planned. He wore a dark-blue suit with a yellow tie that matched her dress, and his natural curls were perfectly styled instead of the devilish mess I was so used to seeing.

The woman had long blond hair that was tied up in a loose, elegant braid. Her light-green eyes practically swallowed the camera whole on her next close-up. Everything about her was perfect, every damn thing. Liam leaned in for a kiss.

I squinted because, for a second, I really did think I was losing my mind. The Liam look-alike on television appeared to match Liam's physical traits to a T, but his style was all wrong and didn't belong to the Liam I knew at all.

Suddenly, everything was starting to make sense—Liam's secrets, the way he'd backed off last night when I'd asked too many questions. He didn't want me to know something about this show. *But why?*

Like a train wreck waiting to happen, I watched the Liam on TV smile at the blond woman in the sparkly dress like he was completely in love with her. The way he stared down at her so adoringly, I wouldn't have doubted if that were the case.

My stomach clenched as my heart squeezed in my chest. *What the hell is going on?* I felt like someone was slicing me with a swift blade, and the pain was slowly setting in, but I couldn't tear my eyes away long enough to save myself. The damage was done. I didn't know what was worse. The fact that Liam clearly wasn't who he said he was, or the fact that it was now excruciatingly clear how much I liked him and all the reasons why I shouldn't.

I knew he'd been keeping something from me. My gut had told me so. The red flags had been flying in front of my face since the day we met. Yet, I would have ignored every single warning if he hadn't been so quick to walk away the other night. I would have slept with him, and I was certain my feelings would only have grown from there.

In my peripheral, I could see that my mom was watching the show too. Liam pulled the blonde onto an empty dance floor while an orchestra serenaded them. He pulled her close, ran his nose along her cheek, then whispered something in her ear that made her smile.

Embarrassment flooded me as I recalled my time with Liam last night, which had been nothing like this. It had been the complete opposite, in fact. I'd never even worn a fancy dress outside of a few high school dances, and they certainly hadn't been as nice as the one on television.

"Have you watched this show?" I asked my mom without taking my eyes off the screen. I hoped she couldn't hear the way my heart rattled and my voice shook.

"Oh yes," she said, her eyes widening.

"What is it?"

"A British reality dating show, but it's just a repeat. The

season ended last week, and boy oh boy, did this Liam fellow make a mess of things. You can never trust a handsome man like that."

I was trying hard not to cry as I whipped my head to catch my mom tsking. "He made a mess of things? How so?"

She nodded at the television. "He started out with thirty women and eliminated all but three, then on the last show, when it came time to pick one, he packed his bags and left them all hanging." She shook her head. "Everyone thought he would pick her." She referenced the woman Liam was escorting into a limo. "He picked out an engagement ring and everything."

A glimmer of hope sparked in my chest. "So, he just decided he didn't want to marry any of them?" That didn't sound too terrible. No one should feel forced to propose.

The shot cut from the date to an interview-type setting, where Liam was speaking directly to the camera. I couldn't hear what he was saying, but that was probably for the best.

"They say he fled Britain too. The media can't track him down. The producers have no clue where he is. He just up and disappeared when clearly he has some explaining to do. He's a coward, if you ask me." She ran a hand over my back. "And you thought Dean was a prick. This guy is the real deal."

My dad cleared his throat behind us. "Well, that's my cue." He stood and squeezed my mom's shoulder, then turned to me. "Staying for a while, honey? I'm baking a fresh batch of scones."

I squeezed out a smile as I rose to my feet. "No thanks, Dad. I've got to get back to the Hogues'. I want to take advantage of all the writing time I have." *And possibly research a certain Liam Colborn.*

"Ah back to the muse." He grinned, his innocence bringing lightness to my heart, even in the circumstances. If my parents only knew that my muse for my current story was the same coward who had just paraded some blonde around on television before breaking her heart.

If I'd had any doubts in my mind when it came to exploring things further with Liam, my heart and mind could now rest easy. Unfortunately, I knew rest was the last thing my heart and mind would do.

15

LIAM

I wasn't trying to stalk Chelsea when I caught her leaving Spill the Tea, but when I saw the look on her face, I thought better than to go to her. She was already angry with me, and I'd already resolved that it was okay for it to be that way. After obsessing over my decision to leave her place the other night without sleeping with her and imagining all the things that would have happened if I had stayed, I knew I couldn't take back how things had ended. Not unless I were to tell her the true reason for my being here.

I also went over all the reasons I should and shouldn't tell her everything—the whole sordid story of my past fuckups—and it became even more clear that I should leave it alone. Why give her my past to deal with when she was so focused on her future? Chelsea was a firecracker of a woman, a woman I wanted desperately to get to know better, but she was also a woman with standards, and I had no right to pretend I was good enough for her.

So, instead of following her on the path she'd taken to get back to the manor, I slipped on my sunglasses and a cap, then entered Spill the Tea. Just like the first day I visited the small tearoom, soft music came through the speakers, and a couple of guests were already seated at a table near the front of the room. Chelsea's mom was at the counter counting money in the register, but as I took another step inside, she looked up and gave me a friendly smile.

It wasn't until I was halfway to her that I heard my voice coming from the televisions positioned around the room. Panic hit me hard. My first thought was that I didn't want to be recognized, but that thought dissolved quickly when I recalled the last time I visited the shop. Between my sunglasses, my clothes, and the fact that I was in Providence, Rhode Island, chances of the tearoom owner recognizing me were slim. They simply weren't expecting my presence. Not only that, but the me who appeared on that television screen was an imposter.

Then my second thought hit me. *Did Chelsea see me on television before she walked out of Spill the Tea?*

The gnawing in my gut increased as I worried I already knew the truth, but I tried to think positively. Maybe she hadn't paid attention to the television, or maybe the televisions hadn't even been turned on until she'd walked out.

Suddenly, I wished I had told Chelsea everything last night, no matter what was going on between us. I didn't want her to find out on her own, and eventually, she would.

I continued cautiously forward, my steps slower than when I'd first come inside, but no one gave me a suspicious glance. If anything, the older woman seemed even friendlier to me than she had the last time I'd seen her.

"Hello, again. I remember you."

"Do you?" I cringed internally, wishing I'd adopted a fake American accent to greet her the first time. Though, I wasn't sure my American accent would be better than that Gwen woman's British one.

Chelsea's mom smiled wider. "I never forget a face. You're the young gentleman who was here earlier this week. Would you like your same order? Earl black with a spoonful of creme?"

I nodded slowly, feeling my exterior thaw for the adorable woman. She reminded me of my own mum back home in London. With her cropped graying hair and friendly demeanor, it was no wonder the regulars loved her, as Chelsea had said.

"That would be nice, thank you."

As she bustled about behind the counter, my gaze looked back up to the television. They were airing one of the last episodes where Francesca and I were finally getting to have some alone time without the cameras present. Up until that point in our relationship, I had thought she was going to be the one I chose in the very end. Except, I hadn't made it that far, not after the conversation we'd had in that hotel room alone, without the cameras watching our every move. It turned out there was more to Francesca than I had yet to witness, which shocked me back to the reality of our situation.

Though I hadn't gotten to know any of the women well enough to propose, the pressure to do just that had my mind spinning and rushing into something that wouldn't have been fair to either of us. I was willing to take one for the team. In retrospect, I would have been an idiot to propose. Luckily, it hadn't come to that.

That night alone with Francesca had been the first time I'd realized how much of a role the cameras had played in the entire eight weeks we'd been getting to know each other. It turned out, she wasn't a sweet, vivacious woman dedicated to finding true love. She had strategized her way to that moment and had thought we were one and the same. She'd wanted me to help her "win."

The moment she had called it winning, I'd known she wasn't in it for the right reasons and she certainly wasn't the right one for me. But what was I supposed to do? Continue to move forward with her? I couldn't. The other women? I couldn't do that either. Not if I were being honest with myself and them. So, I'd walked off the set. And never returned.

"Ridiculous, isn't it?"

I did a double take, pretending I wasn't sure what she was talking about. "What is it?"

The woman chuckled and shook her head. "A reality show, *British Bachelor*. Of course, a man like you wouldn't watch a show like that. Trust me when I say it's a train wreck." Then she waved a hand in the air. "Don't waste your time worrying about it." She pushed forward my tea. "Will that be all?"

Helene was Chelsea's mom's name, according to her name tag. "That will do it." I looked at the register and handed Helene a twenty before grabbing my tea and nodding to her. Apparently, sunglasses still worked wonders as a disguise. "I'm sure I'll be back."

She smiled and waved politely. "Looking forward to it, dear. Maybe my daughter will be here when you come by next time. She lives in the area, and she's single."

Despite the circumstances, I couldn't help the smile spreading on my face. "I'm sure she's as lovely as her mum."

Helene's warm eyes reminded me so much of her daughter's, I felt a buzzing in my chest as I turned toward the door. I wondered if Chelsea had said anything to her mum about me, about the man who was staying at the Hogues' manor. Hopefully she'd left out the fact that he'd wanted to show her his giant willy.

I laughed at my own ridiculous thoughts. How I had any restraint at all to walk away from Chelsea the other night was a mystery. She was nothing like Francesca. She was real, and she was perfect in all the ways I'd gotten to know about her.

I walked out of Spill the Tea with an even heavier heart than I'd walked in with and a determination to sit Chelsea down and talk to her about everything I'd been keeping quiet. She deserved to know the truth—more than the damn British media, more than *British Bachelor* producers, and more than Francesca.

As soon as I reached the house, it was clear Chelsea wasn't home. Her car was gone, and all the lights in the pool area were off. Disappointment sank deep in my gut. Of course she would be gone, and I had no way of getting ahold of her.

I was about to turn dejectedly toward the main house when something white taped to her front door caught my eye. My initial reaction was to leave without glancing at it, but then I realized the note might be for me. I stepped forward, hoping I wasn't massively invading her personal life, and that was when I spotted my name.

Liam,

In case you happen to look for me. I'm visiting a friend for a couple of days. I'll be back when the Hogues return. Didn't want you to worry.

Chelsea

Well, bollocks.

16

I heard their boisterous voices the second I opened my car door early Monday morning. The Hogues were back, bringing an instant smile to my face. Quickening my steps, I pushed my way through the side gate of the house and breezed past the courtyard until I was on the back porch, where the family was all smiling.

Simon and Bridget laughed as the twins, Elizabeth and Eleanor, squealed in Liam's lap. Brendan beamed like the rest of them with his head turned down toward his phone while his fingers danced away on the keys.

I'd taken a much-needed break from the Hogues' residence while I'd digested the news about why Liam was really there. Maisey had let me stay with her and Roger while I spilled all the details of what had been brewing between Liam and me.

She'd always been an amazing friend, but it had been in those moments when I'd started to question all my life decisions that she'd come through hard for me. She'd offered up her study for me to spend my days writing, then she'd dragged me out at night for a full drunken experience filled with wine, laughs, and tears.

We had talked about everything, from Liam to my parents to school to writing. She'd listened with honest, sympathetic, and nonjudgmental ears. It turned out she'd been proud of me for submitting my finished manuscript to an editor, and I'd realized that worrying about her opinion had been a manifestation of my own fear. Once all my confessions were out of the way, we'd googled the hell out of Liam Colborn, which had opened up a whole new can of worms.

Liam's swimming career had been in the public's eye for nearly a decade before he'd faded out of the media, only to return with a vengeance. Not only had Liam been on a television show in the UK, he'd been *the star* of that television show, *British Bachelor*. Or the "Forever Bachelor" as the media reports called him. And apparently, he was a complete jerk. A playboy with zero intention to ever settle down, he seemed perfectly content to make everyone think his intentions were honorable.

All the respect I'd had for Liam felt tarnished, and it wasn't because of the women he'd left behind or the dirt the media outlets had found on him. Liam hadn't even explained his reasons for walking away. He'd simply left England and left everyone there to pick up the pieces of his destruction without any clue as to why.

Seeing him now, smiling and laughing with the Hogues, made my stomach churn with disappointment for a man I had truly started to care for.

"Well, hello there," I greeted on my approach.

Everyone's head snapped toward me at once, including Liam's. I did my best to avoid his heavy stare while the twins gasped, ran to me, and threw themselves into my arms. I hadn't realized how much I'd missed the twin girls until they were hugging me.

"Your vacation was too long," I told them when they released me. Then I placed my hand on the top of Eleanor's head and gasped. "You grew taller."

She giggled, and I did the same thing to Elizabeth and watched her giggle too. Twin giggles, the cutest sound in the world. I wrapped my arms around each of their waists and winked at Brendan, who had finally looked up from his phone.

"What's up, dude? How was your trip?"

His eyes sparkled. Brendan was such a great kid with an appetite for all the experiences his parents were able to give him. I loved that he didn't take those experiences for granted.

"It was the best." He went on to tell me about their trip to see the crown jewels at the Tower of London and the changing of the guard at Buckingham Palace, but then he got distracted again by something on his phone.

I laughed and looked up at Simon and Bridget. "I bet he missed his friends."

"Oh, did he," Bridget said with a laugh. "He's already got plans with Xavier today. I'm going to walk him over in a little bit."

"You must be exhausted," I said. "I thought I'd take the girls out today so you can enjoy some time at home."

Bridget and Simon looked at each other, their eyes sparkling in some silent exchange. Clearly, the idea of being kidless for a few hours excited them.

"I was thinking about taking the kids to the zoo," I added. "If Brendan already has plans, then I can just take the girls. They're having a light show tonight, too, so I imagine we'd get back pretty late, if that's okay with you."

Simon nodded to his wife and shrugged before he turned back to me. "Sold. Why don't you take Liam here too? I'm sure he'd like to check out some Providence sites." Simon looked between Liam and me like he'd forgotten. "You two were able to get acquainted while we were away, I hope."

I felt my face flame, which I tried to hide in my hair as I turned back to the girls, busying myself with making them giggle.

Liam spoke up. "I suppose you could say that. Chelsea was nice enough to show me around downtown Providence. We went to something called—what was that thing called again, Chelsea? Fire Water?"

"WaterFire," I corrected, trying my best to bite the seething anger I felt toward the British man I'd so stupidly fallen for. "I thought it would be a nice thing for me to do since Liam saved me from the cactus poison."

Simon laughed, as he must have remembered that Liam had called him about that. "I'm so sorry, Chelsea. You're never to touch our succulents again, but I appreciate you taking the girls out today. We could use a few quiet moments before we go back to work tomorrow."

I rose to my feet, darting a look at Liam. "Would you like to come with us?"

He stood, rising almost a foot above me as he grinned. "I thought you'd never ask."

Instinct had me laughing as if nothing at all was wrong, but it didn't take long to remember that this banter couldn't happen. Liam wasn't who he said he was, and I wouldn't fall for it again. But as he stood there, I hated the way his breath smelled fresh and minty and how his natural scent was so intoxicating.

For a heartbeat, I remembered the way my arms felt

wrapped around him as he kissed me. A chill rushed over my skin as my lips burned at the memory. I bit down on my smile, kicking my forbidden thoughts to the background, and took the girls' hands in mine. "Great. I'll go get the girls ready now."

17

LIAM

Simon halted me with a firm grip on my shoulder as I started to make my way down to the basement. Bridget was walking Brendan down the street to where his friend lived, and Chelsea was upstairs with the girls. From the second I felt his touch, I groaned inwardly, knowing what would come next.

"If I failed to make this clear," Simon began before I'd even had a chance to turn around, "you are not to get involved with Chelsea. Do you hear me?"

I swiveled to face him, almost hurt by the request. Was I not a grown man who could date whoever I pleased? Not that Chelsea wanted anything to do with me after our last night together. "That's absurd of you to say."

Simon had always felt like another brother to me. After Blake died, he'd often acted more like a parental figure. I knew he was coming from a good place, but I also felt like he was out of line to try to control my life in that way.

"Consider Chelsea my employee," he added. "She's become quite important to our family. I would hate for anything to go wrong between you two. Bridget and I don't have time to deal with whatever fallout would come from that."

"Thanks for the confidence, Simon." My tone was dry, but I was on the verge of getting angry. Did no one in my life believe in me?

Simon sighed and shook his head. "This wasn't how I intended this conversation to go. I love you like a brother, which is why you're here. You're going through a lot of shit back home, and I opened my doors to protect you from it, but I can't have you bringing any of that mess into this family. Do you hear me?"

I nodded, my jaw clenched. "I hear you."

Simon clapped a hand on my shoulder and smiled. "Good. Now that that's settled, have a fun day, but don't rush home." He winked, insinuating he was all too eager for us to leave.

After I had showered and changed, I met the girls in the driveway. Bridget was helping strap the girls into their car seats when I slipped into the passenger seat. Keeping my eyes focused forward, I listened as Bridget kissed the twins on each of their cheeks then waved us off.

Forward, that was where I intended to keep my eyes for the rest of the day. And my plan was working until Chelsea turned on a kids' music station and sang along to the radio with the girls in the back seat. I wanted to watch her, and I might have leaned back slightly in my seat so I could catch her smiling face in my peripheral. I didn't expect my heart to react the way it did with just the slightest glance. How was I going to manage an entire trip to the zoo?

When Chelsea parked the car, I unbuckled my seat belt, and I faltered at my mission. It felt so instinctive, so natural, the way my gaze found hers. My next breath stopped. I wasn't blind to Chelsea's beauty, but there was something different about her now, something more.

She'd thrown her red hair up into a messy ponytail. Her face was clear of makeup, leaving her freckled cheeks and lightly sun-kissed skin exposed. A spot of red touched the tops of her cheeks, telling me she'd recently spent some time outdoors. My mind began to wander down a rabbit hole of where she'd been for the past two days.

Chelsea broke our eye contact to unclick her seat belt and turned to beam at the girls in the back. "Who's ready to see the chimpanzees?"

Elizabeth and Eleanor shot their hands in the air and let out giggle-squeals that were infectious. I couldn't hold back my smile as we all gathered at the front of the car. Chelsea stood between the girls, took each of their hands, and started forward.

I trailed behind them, catching a glimpse of Chelsea's outfit. Black jean cutoff shorts, a long, baggy white tank top tucked in at the front, and bright-yellow sneakers. Our stroll around the zoo reminded me of the day we toured downtown Providence. We'd looked like a couple that day, and we'd kissed like one too.

Shoving all thoughts of Chelsea and what could have been to the back of my mind, I put my energy into helping her with the girls—buying the twins ice cream and hot dogs and helping Eleanor on the pony ride while Chelsea tended to Elizabeth. We laughed at the ostriches trying to mate while the girls laughed at the "giant birds fighting" without a clue as to what was truly going on. I loved watching Chelsea's face turn that deep shade of pink that made it impossible for her to hide her emotions. We stopped to watch the chimpanzee show and kept moving until it started to get late. We fed the girls dinner, and within seconds of crawling into their double stroller, they were fast asleep, leaving Chelsea and me alone on our stroll through the weaving path around the gardens.

We were silent at first, awkwardly so. It was obvious she was planning to keep up the silent treatment, and I hadn't been any better. Of course, with the girls awake, entertaining them had been our number-one priority. Distractions had been easy.

The Japanese garden path ended, and I nodded to an area where we'd watched the elephants play in the water earlier. The animals were much calmer now with the sky beginning to lose its color and the crowds thinning out. I led her to a park bench that overlooked a large pond with a man-made water-fall where an elephant slowly walked by.

She placed the stroller between us as we sat, and I couldn't help but wonder if it was a strategic move on her part.

"You're good with the girls." It was a simple start, an icebreaker of sorts, but it got her to look at me.

"Thanks. I guess I've been nannying for a long time now. Plus, the twins make it easy."

I nodded, agreeing wholeheartedly with that sentiment. "They are happy girls, indeed." More awkward silence passed between us before I finally gave in and turned to her, ready to have it out. "I'm sorry I left your place like that the other night. I should have explained."

Chelsea let out a breathy laugh, her eyes pointed forward while she shook her head. "It's fine, Liam. We'd been drinking. We got carried away. It was nothing."

"It wasn't *nothing*. It was quite the opposite, I'm afraid. It wasn't a mistake either. I never should have agreed with you there."

She looked at me, her eyes searching mine, then she smiled, her face softening. "Well, whatever it was, it can't happen again. I think you know that."

Did I? Because I was selfishly making a list of excuses as to why it absolutely should happen again despite all the reasons why I knew it was wrong. "If it's about my reasons for being here—it's complicated."

She laughed again and leaned back on the bench. "I'm sure it is, Liam. Don't worry. I had no business asking you for your reasons—or anything about your past."

"I like you, Chelsea. I like you a lot. My reasons for being here aren't of the honorable variety. I had planned to keep my secrets. It was why I came here to begin with, but things have changed. I met you, and I think you should know the truth, whether you still like me or not."

She didn't say a word as she stared back at me, her chest rising and falling in slow and deep breaths. "I already know the truth, Liam. You don't need to tell me anything."

And just like that, my worst nightmares were confirmed.

"I saw you on television," she said. "And then I saw what the media said. I know what you did. I get why you're here. I know enough, and I think it's best that we don't get involved any more than we already have."

18

CHELSEA

B rendan was already in the pool by the time I got the twins in their swimsuits and floaties. We stopped by the kitchen so I could pack up some snacks and waters, then we made our way out to meet their brother. As soon as we neared the gate, I heard a pair of male voices laughing, and my gut churned with a flurry of emotions. Liam was swimming with Brendan, and as much as I was excited to see him, I dreaded it at the same time.

Forcing a deep breath and plastering a smile on my face, I rounded the hedge with the twins trailing behind me and opened the pool gate to let them through. "I brought snacks if anyone is hungry."

My shift had started a little after ten today, when Simon was called into work. Bridget was already at the hospital, so the kids were in my care until seven o'clock that evening. We usually loved spending our days at the pool then retiring to their playroom to hang out and watch movies before it was time for me to make them dinner. Bridget would usually come home during their bath time and take over. But today didn't feel like a normal day, not with Liam's eyes on me from the moment I walked through the pool entrance gate.

Brendan, on the other hand, practically jumped out of the pool at the mention of food. The kid could eat anything and everything. It was like he was constantly going through a growth spurt. He opened a block of string cheese and snarfed it before doing a cannonball back in the pool, splashing the twins and me.

I laughed and looked down at my swimsuit cover—a long gray shirt knotted on one side above my knees. Now it was drenched. I pointed to Brendan when he poked his head out of the water. "I'm not above payback, mister. Watch yourself."

He stuck out his tongue then tapped Liam and asked him to race. After a second of hesitation as he took his eyes off me, he nodded and swam to the start line Brendan had set up.

While the guys swam, I walked the twins to the steps and followed them into the pool, instructing them to stay in the shallow end so I could keep an eye on them. They were already decent swimmers, but I made them wear their arm floaties anyway, the fear of anything bad happening on my watch too dreadful to bear.

We were like that for a while, with the boys pairing off, having swimming contests that Brendan miraculously won every now and then, the girls strengthening their skills in the shallow end, and me sitting at the edge of the pool.

"Why aren't you coming in, Chelsea?"

Brendan's question was so innocent, but I couldn't give him an honest answer—that I hadn't expected Liam to be in the pool, and what I was wearing beneath my cover-up was unsightly at best.

"Yeah, Chelsea," Liam added. "Why aren't you coming in?"

Liam's gentle tease was all it took for my neck and cheeks

to heat, but there was no getting out of this, especially not when the twins joined in on the peer pressure. So, with an inward growl, I raised my ass off the pool edge, lifted my cover-up, and tossed it aside, revealing a very unflattering one-piece bathing suit.

The kids had seen me wear this same thing a hundred times, but Liam—I couldn't even look at him. I didn't want to see his reaction to the baggy black-and-pink floral material or the attached skirt that wrapped around my waist and reached midthigh. If our last two encounters hadn't already turned Liam completely off of me, then this would do it right here.

In fact, maybe I should've enjoyed the moment rather than hating it.

Ignoring Liam's eyes at all costs, I let the girls crawl all over me while we swam. When Brendan announced he had to use the restroom, I suggested he take the girls too. Brendan scooped them up on his way out and hustled to the side door of my pool house that led into the bathroom.

"Wow," Liam said as soon as they were out of earshot. "You really know how to pick your swimwear."

I rolled my eyes and turned to face him for the first time since I'd jumped in the pool. Liam's grin was too much to bear. "Yeah, well, it's better than waltzing around in a string bikini with a twelve-year-old walking around. I'm just trying to be respectful."

I hadn't paid attention to the fact that Liam was closing the distance between us until he was almost to me. I backed up, but in less than a step, I was flat against the wall, and his grin widened.

"That's admirable. It really is." The tease in his eyes glimmered in the sun, and my insides felt like they were running in every direction, trying to escape. "But couldn't you have picked something a little less—"

"Hideous?"

He shook his head and lifted a hand to a thick strap around my shoulder. "I was going to say sexy, but if you want to go with hideous, that's fine with me."

I narrowed my eyes, embarrassment swelling up in my chest and heating my body. "Not all of us can look perfect every second of the day."

"C'mon, Chelsea. I'm just taking a piss. You could never look hideous."

He might have been harmlessly teasing, but the flirtation was what sparked my frustration. He was so charming when he wanted to be, and I hated that he was so good at it.

"Is that how you got those girls to fall for you?"

His smile faded as my words sank in.

"Did you flatter them with your lines too?"

"Chelsea—" he started, but I cut him off.

"I'm not a contestant on a dating show, Liam. I didn't sign up for this." I wasn't the type to be passive aggressive. If he hadn't guessed by then, I wanted to make it very clear that I knew what he hadn't had the guts to tell me himself.

Hurt flashed across his features, and his already fading smile dissolved into something darker. "Not everything is as it appears on your television screen, Chelsea. I learned that the hard way. Luckily, you don't have to." With that, Liam pushed himself out of the pool, grabbed a towel from a nearby chair, and headed toward the house.

Later that evening, while the twins were playing in their room, I recruited Brendan to watch them while I started dinner. Once they were settled, I walked out to the kitchen to find Liam standing in the pantry.

"I'm making spaghetti tonight if you're interested," I said, coming up behind him.

He stiffened a little, like he was surprised to hear my voice, but he didn't turn around. Instead, he shook his head and reached for a box of fruity cereal before squeezing by me to get out.

I let him walk by, realizing my olive branch of a dinner offer wasn't enough of an apology for the harsh assumptions I'd made about his past. I hadn't even given him an opportunity to explain his side of the story, and I realized now how wrong of me that was.

In my defense, he hadn't tried to argue either. He'd walked away when he should have told me the truth from the beginning. I was hurt that he'd hidden his reasons for being here from me, and I was disappointed that what I'd thought I was feeling for him just days before all felt like a lie now.

The Liam I'd originally gotten to know wasn't anything like the guy the media had made him out to be. Even as I was researching him and digging up past episodes of *British Bachelor* to watch, none of it sat right with me. But in the end, I knew I owed Liam an apology for my reactions.

After grabbing the ingredients I needed from the pantry, I joined Liam at the island and laid everything on the counter. Liam ignored me while I turned to face him, and he poured out his cereal. I crossed my arms and waited for him to look at me.

When he didn't, I rolled my eyes and sighed. "Liam, let me make you dinner."

He turned to me with bent brows, the milk carton in one hand and the cereal box in the other. "What's wrong with the dinner I'm making?"

I let out a laugh and took a step closer before sliding the bowl farther away from him on the counter. "I'm sorry about

earlier, okay? My assumptions were stupid and probably hurt-
ful, and I'm sorry."

His lips tugged up at the corner. "You think I won't let you
make me dinner because of your assumptions? Trust me, I've
dealt with much worse things as of late. And I happen to
really like cereal." He pulled the cereal bowl back and
completed his mission. When he was done, he retreated out of
the kitchen and down the stairs toward the guest room in the
basement.

19

LIAM

Two nights after the spaghetti versus cereal conversation, I finally broke free from my dungeon and made my way upstairs. It was late, so I knew everyone in the house would be asleep. I'd managed to avoid the redheaded temptress all day, but I was getting restless in my effort to hide out. My stomach was grumbling, and I was craving a little exercise. I would grab some food from the pantry, take a light stroll around the block, then head to bed.

It all seemed like the perfect plan until I made it to the top of the stairs. Chelsea and the twins were sleeping on the sofa in the living room. Elizabeth and Eleanor were on either side of their nanny with their little arms wrapped around her middle. It might have been the only time I'd ever been envious of toddlers.

I almost missed that Brendan was on an adjacent chair until he yawned and stretched before opening his eyes. "What time is it?" he mumbled.

"After midnight, bud. Should we take the girls up to their room?"

Brendan rubbed his eyes and nodded then got up to scoop Elizabeth into his arms while I grabbed Eleanor. Once they were safely tucked in, Brendan handed me the baby monitor. "Chelsea likes to keep that next to her if she's downstairs while they're sleeping."

Then he threw me the peace sign before retreating to his own room.

Back downstairs, Chelsea's eyes were closed, her breathing heavy, and her long red hair was covering half of her freckled face. Even sleeping she was beautiful in the most endearing way.

I walked into the living room and grabbed the remote to turn down the television volume. Then I stood over Chelsea, unable to stop my smile as a cute moan slipped past her throat. I pulled the fallen knitted blanket over her, set the baby monitor on the table in front of her, and started to walk away when her eyes fluttered open.

"Liam?"

I froze, unsure what to do next. I was keeping to myself in the basement for a reason, and it had everything to do with the woman with the long eyelashes and perfect knockers. At least I had imagined how perfect they were while staring at her in that hideous bathing suit the other day.

"Sorry if I woke you. Go back to sleep."

Then she gasped and jerked awake, her head snapping in all directions. "The girls. They were with me when I fell asleep."

I placed my hands on her shoulders and steadied her with my eyes. "They're in their beds, safe and sound. The monitor is there."

Chelsea swiveled to find the baby monitor and exhaled a huge sigh of relief, her palm floating to her chest. "Jeez. Thank you. And Brendan?"

"He went to bed too. Looks like it's just you and me."

She laughed and shook her head. "Yeah, well, I'm sure you have more interesting things to do than to stare at a baby monitor all night."

I shrugged. "You're probably right."

I started to leave again, but a hand slid into mine and squeezed. "No, wait, Liam. Don't go. Sit with me. We can watch a movie."

Bad idea, I told myself. The warning bells were dinging loudly in my mind. But could I really deny her? I hesitated, trying to convince myself to leave. *She's just like the others. Simon forbade it. I'll be going home soon.*

Excuse after excuse played out in my mind, and I found myself rationalizing each one. *Chelsea Banks is certainly not like the others. She's a gem in a world full of fool's gold. And why does Simon get to determine who I can and cannot have a relationship with?* The last time I checked, Chelsea and I were grown adults—adults with needs that could easily be satisfied by each other. Even if it was only for a short while. I'd had casual flings before. Why couldn't I have one with the bombshell nanny who had a brilliant mind and a witty tongue?

"It's just a movie, Liam. But it's okay if you don't want to."

"Is this you trying to make yourself feel better for being so quick to judge me? Who's to say you were wrong, anyway?"

She shrugged. "It doesn't matter. You don't owe me anything. I never should have acted like a jealous ex-girlfriend. I just—I guess I was hurt that I had to hear the truth from the television."

A pang of guilt hit my chest. In retrospect, I completely agreed with the sentiment. "I'm sorry I didn't tell you. It was daft to think I could hide it. As wrong as it was, I quite liked the way you looked at me before."

"I guess we're both sorry then."

I nodded, then a moment of silence stretched between us. She smiled. "Well, I think we can move forward, then."

"Forward?" I didn't want to get my hopes up, whatever she meant by that.

"We have fun together, right?" Her brows raised in question. "You need to be out of the limelight for a while. I need more male inspiration for my book. We might as well make the most of your time here."

And just like that, it was like a weight had lifted off my back. "I love the sound of that."

She tugged on my hand again. "Good. Now sit. I'm going to find us a movie to watch."

I rolled my eyes, feigning annoyance, then dropped down onto the couch next to her, leaving no room between us. She wanted to watch a movie with me? So be it.

I swung my arm around her shoulders, relaxing it on the back of the couch, and waited for her to grab the remote, but she never did. Instead, she turned her body to face me, knee bent in front of her, and leaned in with a curious expression.

"Before I turn on a movie, can I ask you something? It's been bugging me ever since I found out about the show."

I cringed but nodded for her to go ahead. No question regarding *British Bachelor* would possibly be enjoyable.

"What was it like to date a bunch of women at the same time so publicly?"

A chuckle rumbled through me. Of course she had to ask the most general question of them all. I didn't even know where to start. "Do you want to know the truth?"

"I want to know everything. I want to know what it was like."

Her silver eyes gleamed back at me, and I knew I couldn't deny her. "About the same as it would be to date a bunch of women in real life, I suppose, except—picture them all in the same place at the same time, giving you their very best versions of themselves. And in return, you give them the very best version of yourself. You go on these extravagant dates that you could never afford to go on normally."

"Sounds miserable," she chimed in with a playful smile.

I let out a light chuckle before continuing. "You say all the right things so you don't give away too much of yourself to the millions of people watching at home. Suddenly, you start to adapt to the new version of yourself a little too well. You start to believe in the glamour and the false reality. The next thing you know, you're being offered a glass case of engagement rings to choose from because everyone around you thinks you're in love. With who? They don't really care. All the women are beautiful, so why wouldn't you find the one you want to spend the rest of your life with? Hell, even you think you might be falling in love."

All the air in the room felt like it was getting sucked right out, and my body started to shake with the memories that flooded me—the very real feelings involved with the sweeping high and low emotions I'd lived with every single day. I looked her straight in the eye and swallowed. "And then you wake up the next morning."

Chelsea's expression was softer now, all her playfulness gone, her voice just a whisper. "And then what happens?"

I sucked in a slow, deep breath, the words on the tip of my tongue making my heart crash through my chest. "And then you realize that the woman you're two days away from proposing to hasn't once asked you about the meaning behind your tattoos."

Chelsea didn't pry for much longer before she started the movie. She was curious about the type of dates and the extravagant locations where the producers had taken us, but she didn't press for any personal information about me and the girls. I wondered if that was for my benefit or hers.

Perhaps it was smart for us to wade in the shallow end, just past surface level. We knew enough. I didn't keep any secrets, but we wouldn't dig deeper. Still, I couldn't stop thinking about her initial reaction—the anger, the disappointment, the judgment. Who knew what other thoughts were swirling around that beautiful brain of hers?

It was almost two in the morning when the credits of the Adam Sandler movie started to roll, and I turned to see Chelsea sleeping against my side. I gently eased her into a horizontal position, placed my lips on her cheek, and got up to stretch.

Turning to look at her, I didn't want to leave. Not then, not ever. There was something so natural about being with her that I couldn't imagine ever going back to the madness I'd left behind.

Then she shifted onto her side, a quiet moan slipping from her throat as my eyes perused the sleeping beauty's body. One glance was all it took for me to make a decision I told myself I wouldn't regret.

As if it was a sign, my eyes caught on Chelsea's blue note-book. I smiled, picked it up, opened it to the page with a pen sitting between the pages, and started to write her a letter.

20

I t was seven in the morning when the sound of the front door opening jostled me awake. I pulled myself to a sitting position on the couch and stretched my neck, my eyes instantly moving to the baby monitor—not a single movement. The girls would probably sleep in a little bit longer.

I grabbed the monitor and my notebook and walked through the foyer to greet an exhausted-looking Bridget. "Hard night?"

She gave me a look that told me she didn't want to talk about it then lifted the monitor from my grasp. "Still asleep?"

"Yes, but probably not for much longer." I smiled, feeling sympathetic toward the hardworking nurse and mom of three. "Do you need me to stay?"

Bridget smiled with appreciation. "I'll be fine. Simon should be home soon too. I'll scoop the girls up and put them in bed with me. Just be back tonight at five. We have a charity event downtown. We should only be gone for a few hours. Go enjoy your day."

And that was exactly what I intended to do. After taking

my laptop to the pool and writing a couple thousand words, I went inside, showered, and dressed for a walk down to my parents' tearoom.

It felt like a normal day except I couldn't get Liam off my mind—how he'd helped the girls to bed last night just so I wouldn't have to wake up, the way he'd sat with me after I'd asked him to stay, the way he hadn't held back answering questions—and somehow, I'd trusted that he would answer anything I asked, which was one of the reasons I'd stopped.

If Liam was willing to tell me the truth, then he definitely had nothing to hide. And from everything he had told me, it sounded like he'd gotten wrapped in a reality of the show's making, not his own. Of course the producers were mad at him for leaving. He'd walked away from their show. The audience had become invested in the lives of these people and this love story that was never meant to last, but all the audience knew was that Liam had walked away and broken three women's hearts in the process.

I slipped on my shoes and grabbed my notebook from my bed. I always loved stopping in the park and finding a tree to jot notes under before grabbing my tea. As I walked toward my front door, a fluttering sound caught my attention. I looked down to find a folded piece of paper floating to the floor.

That's odd. I didn't remember sticking anything in my notebook.

Bending over, I picked up the piece of paper and unfolded it. At first glance, I saw that it was a letter, then I saw the name, and my heart rate picked up instantly.

I didn't even read the signature at the bottom before I knew exactly who had written the letter. As my eyes scanned the words, I squinted, wondering if I was going crazy or if Liam had just penned a proposition letter.

Dear Chelsea,

I know what you must think of me now that my secret is out, and I can't say I'm not disappointed. I bloody loved that you saw me as someone other than the bloke my entire country has deemed unworthy of love. Maybe I am, but that doesn't stop me from wanting you as desperately as I do.

Before you toss this letter in the rubbish bin, just hear me out.

Soon, I'll need to return home to face the critics—the harsh reminder of the man they all believe me to be, the Forever Bachelor—*and you'll continue to live out your dreams here while nannying the twins. Simon and Bridget are so very lucky to have you.*

All I ask is for one night with you, one night to remove the facade we've exhibited for the past two weeks to mask our true feelings.

Because I want you, Chelsea Banks, more than I've wanted any woman in my entire life, and I dare to imagine that you might just want me too. Even if just for one night.

Liam

By the time I walked back over to the manor to watch the kids, I had reread Liam's letter a few dozen times. I told myself that my second shower of the day had nothing to do with wanting to smell fresh and clean for Liam and everything to do with the fact that I'd sweated a little from doing yoga earlier. The light makeup I wore was purely for the fact that I hadn't worn any in weeks, and it felt good to brighten up a little. Also, the jean shorts and white tank top I'd thrown on had nothing to do with the outfits we'd both worn in downtown Providence the night of our kiss, the night I never should have let him walk out my door.

Simon was with the toddlers in the living room when I walked in the house. The girls were wrestling with their father while Bridget and Brendan laughed from the couch. It almost felt like I was interrupting when Bridget spotted me and waved me over.

"Come in," she said. "We're just about to go to dinner."

I smiled and sat on the couch opposite her while I watched the twins squeal with laughter. "They're the happiest two girls I've ever known."

Bridget threw me a small smile. "I don't know how we'd do any of it without you, but thank you. I like to think we all work pretty well together."

The twins and I walked their parents to the door, where they received one last squeeze, while Brendan sat back on the couch with his Switch.

The moment the door shut, the girls turned to me and jumped. "Hide-and-seek, hide-and-seek."

It was their favorite game, and I always hesitated to play with them without Brendan's assist. I looked over my shoulder, catching his raised brows and understanding stare. He sighed and set his video game down. "Okay, fine, but only a couple of rounds. I told my friends I'd join 'em for a game later."

I grinned, knowing he would cave. He would do anything for his sisters. "Thank you, Brendan. Okay, who's first?"

We played the first round with me on the hunt and the twins hiding with Brendan. I ended up finding them all hiding in the kitchen pantry after a few minutes.

"Too easy," I teased.

They hid again. This time, I found them under the guest bed down the corridor.

"Your turn, Chelsea," the twins squealed.

I laughed and waited until they turned around so I could find the perfect hiding spot. I came to the end of the hallway as the pitter-patter of little and big feet grew louder. I reached for the door of a guest bedroom and pulled myself inside before shutting it quietly behind me. Looking around, I realized I'd never been inside the room before, but I didn't have time to give myself a tour. I was running out of time.

I darted to a closed door in the room, assuming it was the closet, and dashed inside. As I shut it behind me, I realized the room wasn't a closet at all. It was a bathroom, and as I turned around, I noticed something else. Steam was billowing in the air.

Panic rushed through me. Before I could make a mad dash to leave, a figure walked through the fog like a mirage. The next thing I knew, Liam was approaching me wearing nothing but a towel. Water dripped over his tattoos, and his eyes were bright and mesmerizing. I felt rooted in place as he leaned in, his arm lifting until his palm lay flat against the door.

Then he smiled. "Well, hello. Fancy meeting you here."

My heart crashed against my rib cage. "What are you doing here?" I hissed, well aware that I was the one the children were supposed to find. The Hogue kids certainly couldn't find me like this.

Liam's eyes crinkled at the corners. "The basement guest room doesn't have a shower, so I use this one. But I should be asking you that question, love. Is there a reason you decided to join me in the loo?"

My entire body felt hot, and it wasn't from the steam. "I'm hiding from the kids. They're trying to find me." I sucked in a deep breath to calm my nerves. It was a futile effort. "I need to go before they do."

I started to turn, but Liam's free hand caught my waist. "We need to talk." His green eyes practically ensnared mine.

Holy hell, my heart was in my throat, hammering away with no hope of stopping. "Not now," I hissed, desperate to get out of the bathroom before the kids got close enough to figure out that it wasn't just me inside. "Not here."

"Did you get my letter?"

I wasn't sure if I was more afraid to get caught by the kids or face Liam's question. I'd never had a panic attack before, but I was sure this was what it felt like. My skin was all clammy, and my throat went dry while my heart pounded heavily in my chest. "Yes." One simple word, but I could barely make it sound like one. It was all breathy, not at all confident like I'd been feeling as of late. I couldn't lie to the man, but I was uncertain what would happen now that everything was out in the open.

His gaze left my eyes and slid down my body, stopping at the rise and fall of my chest. "You seem nervous. Do I make you nervous?"

I slammed my lids closed, but that didn't stop me from feeling his dominating presence and taking in his powerful scent. Liam wanted me, and I was still trying to figure out all the reasons why it wouldn't work. My mind was blank, my stomach in knots, and all I could think about was just how much I wanted to accept his proposition.

Even if just for one night.

I'd never had anything like what Liam was proposing. *Could I do that? Could I strip down bare for Liam knowing it could only ever be casual?*

A voice on the other side of the door yanked me from my thoughts. "Chelsea," called Brendan.

My eyes shot open, meeting Liam's unfazed gaze. I opened my mouth to respond when Liam's palm covered it, and he held a finger to his lips, telling me to be quiet.

"It's just me," Liam said, his eyes on me while his lips curled up mischievously. "Did you try upstairs?"

My eyes bulged at him incredulously. As soon as Brendan's and the girls' footsteps faded away, I pushed into Liam's chest with my hands. "I'm working, Liam." I hissed my words, still managing to stay quiet. "I can't just disappear on them."

Liam shrugged. "You're playing hide-and-seek. Let them seek for a few more minutes. We need to talk about the letter." His eyes searched mine. "I laid it all out there. How do you feel about it?"

I sighed and leaned against the door. "I feel—confused."

Liam closed the distance again, his fingers tipping up my chin. "You don't look confused, Chelsea. In fact, I think it's the exact opposite."

I swallowed, struggling to find the energy to combat his efforts. He was completely right.

He smiled as if he could read my thoughts. "I can't imagine being this close to you and not pursuing you. I can't imagine going back to London without having ever had the chance with you. I want you, Chelsea Banks, and I dare to imagine that you might just want me too."

Those words. They were straight from the letter. The effects of them sent a tingle throughout my body. "What are you proposing exactly?"

"Did I not make that clear?"

I let out another breath. "You want one night with me? Then you'll be done with me?"

His gaze darkened, and he leaned down to brush his lips against my cheek. "I want to fuck you, Chelsea Banks. And the only promise I can make is that you will come harder than anyone from those romance books you like to read. All I'm asking for is a chance."

His words knocked the wind out of me to the point that I wondered if I was flying. No man had ever spoken to me like that. But from the warmth spreading between my legs, I realized that maybe I had been missing out.

"I don't know if it's a smart idea." I was trying to do the right thing, but I hated that I was potentially sabotaging something I so desperately wanted.

Liam pulled back, shaking his head slowly. "Oh, it's a terrible idea, but it's the best I can think of." He searched my eyes again. "Let me come to your place tonight, and let's see what happens."

After what felt like a million moments, I squeezed my eyes shut, silently praying that I wouldn't regret my next response. Then I nodded.

21

LIAM

At half-past eleven, when I knew everyone in the Hogue manor was asleep, I slipped out the back door of the kitchen and walked across the open foyer, down the side of the house toward the pool gate and let myself inside.

I'd already texted Chelsea, so she was expecting me when I walked up to her door. I didn't even knock before she opened it and whisked me inside. I didn't know what to expect when I saw her, though I'd let a fairly intense scene play out in my mind in the hours leading up to my arrival—one that consisted of throwing her against the wall and kissing the hell out of her before picking her up by her arse and carrying her to the bedroom. But the second I saw her, I forgot all about my lucid fantasies and turned my attention on the now, the present, my reality, not the produced reality of my former world. The differences were not too subtle.

There was a numbness that came along with being the British Bachelor, almost a form of subliminal force that constantly put me at the top of my game, but that wasn't me. I wasn't the man who wore suits to attend fancy affairs or even one who needed the constant publicity to make me feel whole. I wore ripped jeans and T-shirts on the daily, and I much preferred quiet nights to lavish social gatherings—preferably with someone who made life feel effortless, no matter the season, someone who reminded me to value my time rather than rush it. Someone like Chelsea.

All of these reasons played into my restraint, which was why her clothes were still on. I stopped at the door, my gaze slow and sweeping around the room. The lights were dim, with only a tall lamp lit in the corner of her living area along with another light coming from her bedroom. Her small house looked perfectly tidy with every loose article placed where it belonged. I couldn't help but feel like it was a gesture that told me she cared, and my heart grew warmer because of it.

"Do you want anything to drink? Wine. Beer. Water?" She was already walking over to the refrigerator when she asked the question.

It was then that I realized she hadn't met my eyes at all. Alcohol was the obvious choice, but I wanted to have a clear head for tonight, for whatever was about to happen.

"Water would be fantastic."

She nodded and pulled out two bottled waters from her fridge, then walked back to me, still not making eye contact.

"Thank you," I said, biting down on my smile. I decided to see how things went.

She was obviously nervous, but I wanted to make sure it was for the right reasons. I watched her fiddle with the record player near the lamp.

When a familiar tune by The 1975 came on, I walked forward, impressed. "Good choice."

She turned to look at me over her shoulder. "I think I've

listened to their new album about a hundred times in the past two weeks."

"I haven't heard it yet. Turn it up a little?" I stepped around the sofa then sat down on one end, my eyes drifting over Chelsea.

The woman always looked put together. She never had to try, but tonight I think she had. Her hair was down in perfect waves, like she'd just gotten back from the beach. Her skin was bright and flawless, covering up the freckles I had already fallen a little bit in love with. Her sleeveless dress was short and flowy with thin white-and-tan stripes running horizontally from top to bottom. Each of her ears held a small diamond, bright enough to catch my eye but small enough to pull my focus back to her beautiful face. After spending months dating thirty women, all with personal care teams ensuring their makeup was packed on for the cameras, Chelsea was more than a breath of fresh air.

Chelsea took a sip of her water and set it down on the coffee table before turning around to face me. She looked unsure of what to do next but took a seat in the small chair adjacent to me. I wanted to cut through her thoughts for fear she would talk herself out of whatever could happen tonight.

"How is your book coming along?"

I loved the way her eyes lit when I asked her about her passion. Her cheeks pinked slightly, too, and I knew she was excited to talk about it.

"Good. I've written a lot this week. The whole story is coming together. Oh, and the story I submitted to my editor is due back to me tomorrow."

"Can I read more? The sexy bits, perhaps?"

Her blush deepened, and she let out a breathy laugh. "I don't think I could look at you ever again if you did."

It was my turn to laugh. "But you'll publish it for the

world to read? What would stop me from picking it up and reading it?"

Her smile was infectious. "Nothing, I guess. But by then it's already out there, no take-backs."

She was afraid of her own passion, which for some reason, was overwhelmingly endearing to me. I decided to shift the subject. I would love to read whatever came out of Chelsea's brain but only when she was ready.

"So, what happens when you get your edits back? How long until you publish?"

She talked fast through the rest of the editing process, how she would go about getting a cover created, and how everything combined could take weeks before she could actually hit publish. I was fascinated with how much she knew and how familiar her process was to that of any entrepreneur.

"What about you?" she asked when she was done. "Have you given more thought to what your next move will be after you get back to London?"

"I've thought about it a lot actually." I adjusted my position on the couch, wishing I had a better answer for her. "I still love to swim, and I really enjoy coaching Brendan on his technique. I've thought about teaching or becoming a private instructor. I've also thought about starting a tattoo shop somewhere."

I shrugged, knowing my last thought was silly. I couldn't even look at Chelsea as I said it out loud, but when I looked back up at her, her expression made me feel the opposite of silly. I hadn't told anyone else about the dreams I'd been having lately to own my own small business, most of which had been inspired just by being in Providence. I loved the thought of walking to a small shop downtown where my regulars would come for me to draw up artwork for them and get tattooed.

"I think both of those ideas sound perfect for you, Liam. Much different than banking on money from being a social media influencer. Are you ready for the change?"

I swallowed. Hadn't I asked myself the same questions a million times over the past two weeks? "I'm ready to feel fulfilled, so yes, I'm ready for the change." My eyes drifted over her again, my heart quickening in my chest. "I'm ready for a lot of changes."

Suddenly the distance between us was too much. Why was she sitting so far away?

"Have you thought more about getting a tattoo?" I didn't want to assume she still loved the one I'd drawn for her.

She smiled. "I don't know. The temporary still looks pretty good."

My eyes widened, and my trousers tightened. "Can I see it?" I spit the question out without actually thinking about the words first. Chelsea was wearing a dress, which meant if I were to get a peek at it, she would have to—

"Sure." Chelsea rose from her chair and took a couple of steps toward me.

Her shiny and tan legs were right in front of me when I forced my gaze to slide up her body to meet her eyes. "What? Really?"

She shrugged. "I mean, you've seen me in a bathing suit already, and you were there when I got it." She smiled as she took in my reaction. "Unless you don't want to look under my dress. I won't force you."

Panic seized my chest, and my hands practically leapt to her body, gripping behind her knees to keep her steady. If she walked away from me right then, I might weep. "Oh, I'll do it. I just wanted to make absolutely sure I understood what you were offering."

Before I could say another word, Chelsea gripped the

bottom of her dress in both hands and started to slowly pull it up. Inch by inch, my gaze followed the movement. Out of all the experiences I'd had in my life, this was definitely the most erotic.

She halted just before the reveal. My mind had been spinning, trying to guess the color of her panties. When she didn't go farther, I looked up into her eyes again and watched her take her next deep breath.

It was like she wanted to be brave but faltered slightly. That breath signaled a line we had yet to cross, a line she was less than an inch from letting me explore. This time, I wasn't walking away from the opportunity.

Her body shifted slightly, and I realized she was lifting her arms again. The anticipation would kill me. I hadn't even glanced back down yet, and I was already harder than I'd ever been in my life.

My gaze fell to find silk black panties, the waistband of them thick so only the top of the tattoo peeked out over the fabric. An internal growl ripped through me, my hunger for this woman on a completely new level. Something beastly was set to emerge, and I had no idea how I would control it.

Without thinking, I moved my hands up her silky-smooth legs. I had to bite my bottom lip in an attempt to contain the trouser snake below my waist. When I reached her panties, I let one hand drift to the top of her waistline before I made eye contact with her again. "May I?"

She nodded, her smile gone but her shallow breathing an acceptable indication of my welcoming touch. I swallowed and focused on the little ink I could see of the tattoo. I pulled one side of her panties down over her hip so I could get a full glimpse of my creation tattooed on the woman in front of me.

I moved with instinct, tracing over the tattoo as I remembered how fast my hand had moved that day. With Chelsea as my inspiration and with my passion for art and ink as my guide, it had come together like magic. As I looked at it now, no words could describe the emotions swirling inside of me.

"You're right," I said, my voice low. "It still looks good." I continued to trace the design down to the bottom, where I knew I was coming close to another part of Chelsea I so desperately wanted to see.

My finger slipped below the fabric, dragging along her skin and moving farther away from the tattoo. It was a tease, a question, and when Chelsea didn't flinch or jerk away, I looked up to find her eyes falling closed.

Permission granted.

22

My eyes fell closed as his touch sent a wave of electricity through my body. I was still gripping the bottom of my dress, giving him access to a part of me I wanted him to take without question. No more questions, just action.

I inched forward slightly until I felt his knees on either side of my legs and his hot breath on my skin. I dared a look down in his direction, finding his blazing eyes back on mine.

Holy shit. I couldn't take it anymore. I didn't know why this beautiful man was here with me or why he looked like he would devour me slowly just to torture me in the best possible way. All I knew for sure was that I wanted him and that he wouldn't leave this pool house without knowing it.

He continued to graze the skin beneath my panties, slowly, cautiously, but also easing his way down, like he was testing my reactions. I wouldn't give him any reason to stop.

I lifted my dress over my head, revealing my bra, and I tossed the garment to the chair I'd just been sitting on. When I turned back to Liam, he let out a heavy breath, slammed his lids closed, and moved his head so it was resting on my stomach.

"Holy hell, woman. You'll be the death of me."

I bit down on my smile, flutters coming alive inside of me as heat spread between my thighs. "Not if you kill me first."

When he looked at me again, it was with an intense glare that had my heart pounding fiercely in my chest. "I can only promise to try."

Keeping his eyes locked on mine, he peeled my panties from my body, inching them down around my legs until they fell to my feet. His mouth hovered over my tattoo before he pressed his lips against it. I shivered at the touch, and he gripped the back of my thighs.

Liam ran his lips against my skin, traveling away from the tattoo until he was right above my bare mound. "You're so sexy." His voice was gravelly and hot on my skin as he spoke. "And sweet." His mouth lowered. "And so bloody hot."

His tongue slipped out and swept between my legs, which were only marginally parted. Liam must have realized the same thing because he scooted back as far as he could on the couch then patted the edge of the couch on either side of him. "Put your knees here." Then his eyes flashed to mine, his intent clear. "Spread your legs around me."

With shaky muscles, I moved forward, dipping one knee onto the couch then the other, with my hands straight down by my sides. When his thumb touched my clit and started to rub, I knew I wouldn't be able to hold myself up.

My hands wrapped over Liam's shoulders as he kissed my belly, all while his thumb ran circles around my sensitive bud. A second later, his other hand joined in on the action as he ran a finger along the length of my slit, all the way to my ass, and back to my front. The motion was slow and agonizing as I shook above him.

"Liam," I begged when the sensations were getting to be too much.

I didn't have to elaborate, and I didn't have to wait much longer for two fingers to push inside me. My lids shot open at the intense pressure.

"Come closer," he demanded, his pace set as he pulled me onto his lap and took my mouth with his.

We became heated breaths, tangled tongues, and grazing teeth as I moved around his magical fingers fluttering deep inside me.

His lips dragged from my mouth to my neck as his thrusting fingers quickened their pace. He wanted me to come for him before he'd even stripped off a single article of clothing. Suddenly, I was eager to meet my climax, eager because it meant I was that much closer to seeing Liam come alive too. Just the thought of our naked bodies tangled together dizzied my mind.

The moment I felt the start of my orgasm, it was like a stick of dynamite had just been lit, the flame teasing me as everything at my core heated until its final detonation. My moan was soft as my entire body absorbed the effects with every aftershock that came. I fell into Liam, his fingers sliding out of me, leaving a trail of my sticky wetness before he cupped the nape of my neck and pulled me to his mouth for another heart-stopping kiss. With his fingers gone, I could feel him hard beneath me—rock-hard and practically throbbing to get inside me.

Then his mouth moved to my ear as his free hand gripped my ass. "Consider that the hors d'oeuvre in a five-course meal," he rasped. He lifted his hips, the thin fabric of his sweats leaving little to the imagination.

I was still coming down from my high when he unsnapped my bra, and it slid down my arms. He lifted the fabric from my skin and tossed it to the floor, his eyes glued to my heaving breasts.

"*Fuck me.*" He cupped me, filling his palm with me while his eyes rolled up and his head fell back on the couch. "Holy shit, woman. You're unbelievable."

A smile lifted my cheeks at the compliment, and I shifted on his lap to get a better feel of him. "You haven't even fucked me yet."

His lips curled into a smile. "The first few courses are just a warm-up to the main event."

I laughed lightly, my head still spinning from my climax. "I don't think I've ever had a five-course meal."

His eyes widened in a challenge. "I'm happy to introduce you."

My finger slid against his bottom lip. I wanted nothing more than to place it between my teeth and suck. "What course comes next?"

His gaze darkened as his brows lowered. "The appetizer."

Before I knew what was happening, Liam scooped me up into his arms then laid me down on my back. In a quick move, he swiped his white T-shirt over his head, and it met the floor, which was quickly becoming decorated with our wardrobe. His chest was smooth, just like my pussy, like he'd waxed it for the occasion. I'd never had sex with a man who looked like Liam—perfectly cut, his strength undeniable as I ran my eyes over the cut of his chest and abs.

He cupped my breast again while he kissed my mouth, this one rough, unlike before. Then he moved to my neck, his teeth grazing my soft skin until my eyes rolled back into my head. *Holy shit*, it was like my entire body was on fire.

When his mouth moved to the breast he'd been cupping, a guttural moan slipped past my throat. Liam took the sound as an invitation to suck hard on my nipple before adding his teeth. It was just a pinch, but it was enough for me to gasp in surprise at the sensation. No one had ever done that to me before.

He flicked his tongue against me before sucking again and finally sliding down to where my thighs parted. He didn't tease my center as he had before. His tongue swiped at my entrance as his hands gripped my thighs and squeezed them around his head.

While I'd never had a five-course meal, I'd eaten plenty of appetizers, none of them at all this satisfying. Liam went straight for the kill. The pressure built so fast within me that I tried everything I could think of to stop my impending orgasm.

His tongue delved into me as he swiped each time, his pacing quick but steady as I started to quiver beneath him. I cupped my breasts, needing something to hold onto as he devoured me whole. The fire he'd already lit inside me built to an inferno, blasting through my body at a rate I could no longer control. His hands slid under my ass and gripped it hard while his final suck had me coming so hard, my entire body convulsed beneath him.

"Please tell me the main course comes next." I gasped with my words, afraid I would never be able to regulate my breathing again.

He chuckled as he rose from between my legs. "Nope. One more course to go." Liam pulled me off the couch, tugged me close, and breathed his hot breath in my ear. "Take me to your room."

I met his intense gaze before nodding and stepping backward with him still pressed against me. Once inside, we stood at the foot of my bed while my heart pounded chaotically in my chest. I looped my finger into the top of his sweats and tilted my head. "I think you're a little overdressed for this meal."

He cocked his head, his smile widening. "What are you going to do about it?"

Swallowing, I bottled up my nerves and slid my eyes down to his drawstrings, where my finger rested. Why was I so damn nervous to see a guy naked? It wasn't like it was my first time, but in a way, it felt a whole lot like it. My head felt light. My stomach was doing somersaults, and I had to suck in a slow breath so I didn't sound shaky.

Confidence, Chelsea, I scolded myself. After a short exhale, I used both hands to grip the top of Liam's sweats and slid them down over his boxer briefs. I peeled his briefs away next, inch by inch, until his cock sprung free right next to my mouth. My eyes widened, and for a second, I thought I might lose my nerve. Without thinking twice, my right hand wrapped around it. I was entranced by his size. Now I was intimidated for a whole new reason. How was I supposed to fit that *thing* inside me?

When I dared another look at Liam, he'd lost his smile and had replaced it with a hooded gaze.

"Chelsea, I'd like to introduce you to Willy, our dinner guest."

23

I almost expected Chelsea to shy away from me after her introduction to Willy. Instead, the gleam in her eyes told me she was up for the challenge. Her hand was already wrapped around me when she looked back down and flicked her tongue out to lick her lips.

The wait was almost too much—I watched her while she gazed at my todger like she was contemplating her plan of action. Would she try to fit it in her mouth all at once? Would she work her way down to the base slowly just like I'd tortured her? Who knew? I would probably come as soon as she wrapped those pretty pink lips around me.

It was her tongue that made the first contact, swirling the tip before her mouth wrapped around it and sucked. Her lips smacked as she pulled away and dove right back in. Flattening her tongue on the underside of my base, she applied pressure against the vein. When her light-blue eyes snapped to mine, she started her ascent, running the tip of her tongue all the way up and wrapping her lips around me again, this time taking me deeper into her throat.

"Bloody hell, woman." I gasped as I placed my hands on the back of my neck, doing everything I possibly could to contain my pending orgasm.

She started out almost hesitant but grew more confident by the second. Now, she was too good. Her hot mouth sent chills through my body. When her small hand started to stroke me as she took me until I hit the back of her throat, I lost all control. My climax came quickly, powerfully, and I managed to pull away from her mouth with enough time to decorate her neck and chest with my excitement.

"Jesus fucking Christ," I growled.

I'd expected to come quickly. While I'd wanked myself off plenty of times, mostly to thoughts of Chelsea in a bikini, it felt like ages since I'd last slept with a woman. When I finally had Chelsea beneath me, I wanted it to last, hence the massive amounts of foreplay until the main course, which was coming up next. The way her eyes sparkled as she looked back at me, she knew it.

She sat on the bed, her naked body the sexiest I'd ever seen. With her light-pink nipples, her freckled skin, and her long red hair a tangled mess around her head, she was a vision I knew I would never get enough of.

"Don't move," I demanded with a point of my finger.

I walked to the bathroom to clean myself. Returning with a towel, I swiped off the droplets on her chest. Biting down on my smile, I tossed the towel aside and pushed her onto her back while placing my knee between her thighs and resting my palms on either side of her.

"You think you can handle me?" It was a tease, playing off Chelsea's initial reaction to seeing me, and it made her smile too.

"I think I handled you just fine already."

Touché. I chuckled and leaned in to kiss her in what I'd

intended to be a quick peck before moving down her body again, but that wasn't what happened. Once my lips touched hers, I wanted to memorize them, the soft lines and steep curves of her cupid's bow. I wanted to explore her cool, minty mouth, the way her body reacted when I pulled her bottom lip between my teeth and sucked.

It seemed the feeling was mutual. While our kiss was agonizingly slow, our intensity grew by the second. And by the end, we were a pile of tangled limbs, hasty tongues, and bruised lips. If it hadn't been for Willy waking between us, I probably never would have stopped.

In a quick maneuver, I rolled so my back was on the bed and Chelsea was above me. Her hair fell over her shoulder, and her palms pushed into my chest. It was like we didn't need to speak another word. I reached between my legs and stroked my length slowly, hardening.

"Willy is up for the challenge, I see." She grinned, making me jerk in my fist.

"Oh, he is, love." Then I looked at her wet opening and bit my lip. "More than you know."

Once we were aligned, she eased her body down around me, her mouth widening as a not-so-subtle moan shook her throat.

"F-uuuck."

She quaked as she slid down around me, her muscles squeezing me like a death grip. Meanwhile, my breath was caught somewhere in my chest as my glance fell to her temporary tattoo. Not only was a gorgeous woman on top of me, but she was wearing my art.

A feeling of possession swarmed through my chest, my gut, my soul. That was when I realized that I wanted to call her mine, not just for one night. I wanted Chelsea Banks for as long as she would keep me.

My hands slid up her legs to reach her arse, and I gave it a good squeeze before lifting my hips to take her deeper.

My chest swelled when I saw the first bead of sweat form on her brow. She hadn't even started riding me, but I knew my length was more than she'd anticipated. Even after going down on me, her body had to acclimate, and I thought I might go crazy waiting for her to do so.

I wanted to growl, scream, flip her over, and ram every last breathy moan from her beautiful body. I would let her take her time getting used to me, but after that, I had every intention of quickening the pace and fucking her without mercy. Patience did not feel like it was on my side in that moment, and I was getting ready to lose my mind.

With each nudge of my hips, she fell deeper and deeper until our bodies finally collided, and her lids fluttered closed.

"Holy shit, Liam. Your willy is so… *girthy*."

As turned on as I was, I laughed at her compliment. At least, I thought it was a compliment. I'd certainly take it as one. "Yeah, well, your sally will get on just fine once you start moving." I squeezed her bum.

"Did you just name my vagina?"

I groaned as her laugh shook her body. "I didn't realize I'd done that, but I do like the sound of it. Your Sally, my Willy— it makes for a rather good team, don't you think?"

She breathed out a sigh and circled her hips. "I'm more than happy to find out."

In the next instant, our smiles were gone as Chelsea started to move above me. Clearly, I wasn't the only one who wanted to put forth their best effort. She eased up and down my length like a champ, using my chest as her leverage so she could quicken her pace.

Every now and then, she would come down to my base, and her eyes would roll into the back of her head like she was seconds from coming. The fact that I didn't know when she would let go only riled me up more, bringing me closer to my own release.

I sat up, wrapping an arm around her waist while slipping a finger between her bum cheeks. Chelsea moaned as I applied pressure, then she rode me even faster while her breathing stuttered between her frequent high-pitched moans.

Meanwhile, my own climax was intensifying to a point where my head started to fog while my heart felt like it would punch straight through my chest.

"Liam," she finally cried.

A burst of adrenaline pumped through me as I slammed my hips up into her, causing her head to fly back as I fucked her. My lids slammed closed, making everything go dark while my other senses intensified. I could hear every single sound that slipped out of her pretty throat as I moved her above me. I could smell the erotic scent of sweat and sex as our mouths collided, and I could feel her pussy as it convulsed violently around me. My own orgasm shot through me, filling her with everything I'd promised to give her, knowing that it would never be enough, and hoping that she felt the same.

24

When I walked into the Hogues' kitchen the next day, Liam was leaning against the island, eating a bowl of puffy cereal. He looked up and raised a brow when he saw me, the spoon almost to his mouth. "Simon just left. He said you'd be here soon. Guess my shift is over."

He flashed me a grin before taking a bite, and as tempted as I was to become mesmerized by his wet lips and strong jaw, I was distracted by what he'd just said. Simon had already left for the day, which meant the kids were in Liam's possession.

I looked around the room to find the twins quietly sitting at the dining room table, drawing all over it with crayons. "What the—" I dropped the groceries I was holding at my feet and rushed over to them before they could do too much damage.

As I got closer to the girls, my panic deflated in my chest, and I halted behind them. They weren't drawing on the table, not directly anyway. They were drawing on a large sheet of packing paper that covered the entire area. The girls' eyes were already wide on me after hearing me yell. The poor things looked frightened, like they'd done something wrong.

I let out a slow sigh, rubbed the girls on their backs, and pushed out a smile. "False alarm. Keep up the good work."

A chuckle floated up behind me. "Are you okay?"

I did a slow pivot to face Liam.

For so many reasons, I was not okay, not in the least. At some point in the middle of the night, Liam had sneaked out of the pool house. I shouldn't have woken up at five in the morning to a sinking heart, especially since he'd done nothing wrong. It was what we'd agreed to—one night. And I'd gotten far more than I'd bargained for—a marathon of sex, more orgasms than I could keep track of, and the sight of the British Bachelor himself naked and sweaty and completely tuned into me.

The night was a lot of things, least of all disappointing, but that was exactly how I'd felt after tossing and turning once I realized I was alone in my sex-scented sheets. *Ugh. I can't think about last night right now.* My eyes flickered to meet his, and my neck and cheeks immediately warmed. "I didn't see the drawing paper, and I panicked a little."

"A little?" Green eyes shone back at mine, Liam's cocky lips tipping into a bigger smile. "And here I thought you'd be relaxed today." He shrugged. "Not sure why." Then, like an asshole, he winked and leaned down to pick up the bags I'd dropped.

I met him at the counter as he handed me items one by one and stared down at them curiously. When he reached the bottom of the first bag, he tilted his head. "Why are you buying Simon and Bridget's groceries?"

I smiled. "I have a credit card for stuff like this. Bridget asked me to pick up dinner, and some of the stuff is for me for when I'm here and can't get to the pool house."

He nodded and started to unpack the next bag, stopping at the two balls of rolled-up dough. "What's this?"

Biting down on my lip, I took them from him and set them on the counter. "Dough. I'm making pizza with the kids tonight."

"You really like pizza, don't you?"

I laughed, feeling my cheeks redden more. I hadn't even thought about it until he said that. "What's wrong with pizza?"

"Nothing at all," he said, raising his hands above his head. "I like learning things about you. That's all." His eyes darted to where the twins still sat calmly coloring away, then he leaned in, brushing his scruffy cheek against my smooth one. "Like the way you sigh after you come."

Oh my God, he did not just say that. I narrowed my eyes, ready to let him have it, but Brendan chose that moment to come running into the kitchen.

"I'm so hungry," Brendan said before looking over the contents of my recent grocery trip. After a quick scan, he grabbed the bag of Hawaiian rolls and dashed back out of the room.

Liam closed the gap between us again, this time placing his hands on either side of me on the counter, caging me in. When I looked up, his face was right there in front of mine, so close I could practically feel him inside me. Obviously, not literally. But the feel of Liam's Willy inside of my Sally was not something I would soon forget.

"I'd like to learn more about you tonight, if that's all right."

His voice was quiet, but that didn't stop the rasp of it from tingling up my spine. "I think you learned enough last night. One time, remember, Liam? Or did my performance wipe your memory?"

He grinned and bit down on his bottom lip as laughter rocked him. "You give great blow jobs, love, but no one has ever managed to give me amnesia from one, not even you."

I scoffed and tore my eyes from his. I couldn't even look at the man without wanting to replay every second of our night together. "Then you remember our deal. There are reasons why we shouldn't repeat it."

"And what are those?" he challenged, narrowing his eyes.

I let out a laugh. Liam was unbelievable. He was really going to make me say it. "Because," I started with all my energy on the word. "Neither of us can afford to start something, not with you heading back to London soon."

His brows pushed together like he was confused. "Isn't that why we should spend more time together? We hang out. We have fun. It doesn't have to be a thing, Chelsea."

My heart sank, but I pushed aside the disappointment I felt at his choice of words and shook my head. "That's the problem. If we keep doing this, it will become a thing *for me*." I searched his eyes, wanting him to understand. "I can't just sleep with someone without getting attached, Liam. And—" My gaze flickered down as a sudden bout of bashfulness overtook me. "I think you're someone I could get attached to quickly."

If anything would scare away a man who only wanted to be a casual partner, it would be the truth. I inhaled a deep breath and looked back up to find his throat bobbing while he gazed over my shoulder in a daze.

When he finally met my eyes again, he shrugged, his expression completely nonchalant. "Fine. No more Willy for you. But we can hang out again, right? Like before?"

I laughed at his reference to his penis before settling into a smile. "Is that possible after what you did to my Sally last night?"

His eyes widened in mock surprise. "Of course it's possible. We'll just hang out without all the touchy-feely stuff."

He was so calm about never touching me again. It irked me more than I wanted to admit. "I mean, I guess we can still hang out." An internal battle raged inside of me, and I was desperately trying to stay strong.

"Really?" His grin was too irresistible to ignore.

My insides practically purred as I stared back at him, cursing myself for falling for his charm.

"So, tonight? There's somewhere I want to go, and I want you to come with me." His hopeful smile tugged at my heart.

"I'm working all day. I'll probably be tired." I swallowed. It took every ounce of strength to not jump on his offer. "Where do you want to go, anyway?"

Liam bit his bottom lip and pushed off the counter. "You'll find out tonight."

Panic shot through me like a cannon. "I didn't agree to come."

He winked. "You didn't disagree either."

"Liam," I scolded. He wasn't listening to me at all.

He sighed, a smile still playing on his lips. "An innocent night out, that's all I'm asking for. Just consider it." Then he walked off, leaving me to ponder his request while tending to Elizabeth and Eleanor for the rest of the day.

I joined the girls at the table, but their attention span for coloring was just about at its limit, so we cleaned up and went to their room for a tea party in their pink tent. During tea, Elizabeth decided all the stuffed animals and dolls should join in on the fun. Meanwhile, Eleanor pulled me over to her closet to help her try on princess dresses. The girls and their imaginations always astounded me. Hours passed, and we'd done nothing but play pretend games and speak in funny voices, giggling throughout the day.

"Chessy, help." Elizabeth bounced over, her white puffy dress on upside down, and I laughed before helping her put it on the right way.

"Chessy, I want a dwess too." Eleanor's jealous eyes were wide on her sister as she left her tea party to look in her closet.

"How about this pretty blue one?" I pulled the dress out of the closet and turned to look at the three-year-old, whose face was scrunched up in disapproval.

"No, not dat one."

I put it back and tapped my lips, trying to play along with her wardrobe selection, then I gasped. Plucking a yellow dress from the closet, I turned back to Eleanor and squatted to her level.

Her eyes were almost as big as her head, and she clapped with glee. "Yes."

I helped her put it on over her clothes then took pictures of her and her sister to send to Simon and Bridget.

When it was time to make dinner, the girls insisted on keeping the dresses on and taking the tea party downstairs. So, we made homemade pizza with princess dresses on and teacups in front of two of our stuffed dinner guests, who the girls managed to entertain the entire time.

Brendan and Liam, who had been playing video games in Liam's room, walked in at just the right time. The kitchen was a mess. Flour and pizza sauce was everywhere, in the girls' hair, on their clothes, and all over the counter. Laughing, I picked them up from their stools and set them down in front of Brendan. "Do you mind getting them cleaned up for dinner? I'm going to pop the pizzas in, then we can eat in twenty minutes."

"Sure thing," Brendan said with a grin, then he looked down at the girls and laughed. "I hope that sauce comes out."

I made a face, hoping the exact same thing. "I'll throw them in the wash to try to salvage them."

"Don't worry about it," he said, lifting the girls into his arms. "I'll do it."

And with that, the three of them made their way up the stairs, leaving a snickering Liam behind.

I swiveled around, narrowing my eyes in a glare as I walked over to put the pizzas in the oven. "What's so funny?"

He crossed his arms and leaned against the stove, then he pointed at my breasts. "You've got a little something on you."

I looked down to find the black fabric over my chest covered with flour in the shapes of my breasts. "Geez," I hissed before grabbing a cloth from the counter and swiping at it until it looked clean. "Thanks for the warning."

Liam was grinning, his eyes still focused on the spot I'd just cleaned, when I smacked him with the towel, forcing his eyes back on mine. "My face is up here."

His perfect smile rested on his face. "Did you decide on tonight?"

"What?" I felt flustered. Had I thought about taking Liam up on his offer to go somewhere tonight? All damn day. But as much as I wanted to, I couldn't let Liam distract me. "I need to get some writing done tonight." The moment the words were out, I wanted to take them back. I hated the disappointment that flashed in his eyes. "But—" I started again. "I have a day off two days from now, if you want to do something then."

His face lit up at my suggestion. "Really?"

"Can you handle waiting that long?" I teased.

Liam's eyes narrowed, but his smile remained. "I think I can manage." Then he extended a hand between us, gesturing for me to take it.

I mustered up as much confidence as I could, then I

slipped my hand in his. I couldn't ignore the current between us, and by the way Liam's gorgeous green eyes glowed back into mine, I knew he could feel it too.

"Two days, Miss Banks, then you're all mine."

Even words that should have sounded innocent made me warm all over. Why did I feel like Liam already had zero intentions of keeping things in the friend zone? And why did that simple thought thrill me to my core?

25

LIAM

Two days felt a hell of a lot longer than I'd initially imagined. What started out as a casual test of will turned into complete and utter agony as I caught glimpses of Chelsea while she played with the girls, heard her soft laughter from down the hall, or stepped outside to the sound of water splashing from the pool and knew she was there, wearing that hideous bathing suit of hers.

Somehow I did it. I managed to steer clear of my sassy redhead while waiting two whole days to take her out. *As friends.* I had to keep reminding myself about that last bit. And while she'd mentioned getting together tomorrow, I planned to surprise her tonight, long after her shift ended.

After parking the rented motorcycle down the street instead of in the Hogues' driveway, I tried to keep as quiet as possible. I sneaked in through the pool gate and knocked on Chelsea's side door until she opened. A light flicked on, then an eye peeked through the blinds before I heard a click on the other side of the door. It opened to a pissed-off Chelsea.

"What are you doing here, Liam? You scared the hell out of me," she hissed, her eyes furious at my surprise visit, but I couldn't stop smiling.

"It's been two days. A deal's a deal."

Her jaw dropped, then her hands moved to her hips. "We made plans for *tomorrow*, not tonight."

"Well, I have a surprise tonight, so get dressed."

Chelsea looked down—and so did I—at her headlights poking through a silk white tank. "Or we could stay here." My gaze slipped down farther to find her in black panties that had me stepping back and shoving my hands into my pockets. "Bloody hell, you had to be wearing that?"

Her arm flew over her chest, and she glared up at me. "I wasn't expecting company."

"What were you doing?"

It was a simple question, but by the silence that followed and the guilty look in her eyes, I knew exactly what she'd been doing. Now that I was studying her closely, I recognized a glow to her I'd only seen one time before—the night we'd shagged like animals for hours.

"Well then," I said before clearing my throat. I wasn't one to get uncomfortable around a lady, especially an attractive one, but the longer I stood in front of Chelsea, the dirtier my thoughts became. Surprisingly, that wasn't what tonight was about. "I hope you were thinking of me at least."

She let out a half groan, half scream before pulling me inside and shutting the door behind me. When she turned around, I got an eyeful of her bum, bare with just a slip of material between her cheeks.

"I'll get dressed."

Stifling my groan, I stepped behind her into her bedroom and hopped onto her bed. Leaning against the headboard, I rested my hands behind my head and bit my lip while I watched her peruse her closet. She reached for a blue sundress first then turned to me for approval.

I shook my head. "As much as I love you in those dresses, you'll want to put on some long pants tonight."

She narrowed her eyes then leaned down to open a drawer beneath her hanging clothes. I shifted against my tightening trousers, my bum hitting something hard when I moved. Glancing down, I found a pink U-shaped object made of silicone with gentle ridges across the top. I picked it up, running my thumb over one end of it before realizing what I was touching.

"Is this what I think it is?" I held up the device while Chelsea's eyes shot up in surprise.

"Oh my God, put that down." She charged for the bed, throwing her leggings to the side as she climbed toward me, her face heavily flushed with embarrassment.

I couldn't stop laughing as my question was confirmed. I held the vibrator high in the air as she mounted me, her jubblies bouncing in her wild rush to grab for it.

"I hate you," she growled as her hips bounced off my lap to reach for it again.

"You don't hate me, love." My free hand slid up her leg, around her body, and over her bum cheek. I pressed her down on my lap and moved my mouth to her neck, kissing her there before darting my tongue out for a taste. God, I'd missed her, her taste, her smell. Her entire essence wrapped around me like a warm winter blanket.

Her breathing was still heavy, but she stopped fighting as she moved against me, her knickers to my trousers. When a buzzing sound lit the air, she froze while I smiled wide. I'd found the power button on her vibrator and switched it on.

"How about I help you out with this before we leave?"

Chelsea sat back on my lap, her eyes glazed over and staring at my hand that held her special toy. I moved it closer, allowing her the chance to refuse my offer, but she didn't move an inch. I aimed for her leg first, running it up her thigh and over her hip, then to her stomach. The moment the vibrator touched her belly button, her abs shook so hard I thought I might come from osmosis.

She sucked in a deep breath, her legs tightening around me. I ran the vibrations over her abs a little longer before working the device up beneath her top and over her breasts. Her eyes slammed shut, and she moaned as I circled her nipples slowly one at a time. I was having too much fun watching her as I teased her slowly. Willy, on the other hand, was not impressed. He twitched beneath her, aching each time she moved against him like she was trying to get herself off.

When I couldn't stand it anymore, I pushed her top up to reveal her breasts. Her pretty pink nipples were swollen and hard and ripe enough to taste. My mouth covered one, and I moaned as I slipped the vibrator between Chelsea's legs and settled on the fabric above her clit.

I pulled back to watch her eyes flutter closed as her knees quaked around me. Usually, when I gave, I had every expectation of receiving. Not this time. I found myself quite fascinated with the redheaded vixen as she lit up with my touch, moaning and quivering as she came.

Tossing the pink toy, I cupped Chelsea's head and pulled her to my mouth, slamming her to me with my own desire swirling beneath my waistline. "Good heavens, woman," I growled between kisses. "How am I supposed to walk after that?"

She laughed, the sound airy in comparison to her moans a

moment ago. "Did you really have plans for us, or was that just a ploy to get into my bed?"

I grinned and grabbed her by the bum, lifting her off my lap. "Come and find out."

26

CHELSEA

We walked a few hundred feet down the sidewalk before I spotted it sitting there, all shiny black and chrome. "Please don't tell me you're going to make me get on that thing." That was when I saw them—two helmets hanging off the handlebars, confirming my fears.

Liam chuckled when he saw my reaction and tugged on my hand, pulling me closer. "Oh, come on. I rented it for the rest of my visit. You have to ride with me."

It wasn't that I was afraid of motorcycles. I used to go dirt biking with my friends when I was in high school. I had just realized there was more to Liam that I didn't know. "Do you even know how to drive this thing?"

"I got the motorcycle here, didn't I?"

I supposed he had a point.

He plucked a black helmet from the handlebar and pushed it to my chest. "What's the matter, Chelsea? Afraid of a little wind in your hair?"

"Hardly." I grabbed the helmet and placed it over my head while I took in his outfit with a smirk—white shirt, zip-up hoodie, ripped black jeans. It was the same outfit he'd had on when I'd first spotted him at Spill the Tea, but it all made sense now. Liam looked like a walking, talking stereotype—the bad boy Brit with seemingly nothing to lose. And while this was the version of him I'd gotten to know well, the Liam from back in London—who the media was having a frenzy over— was someone completely different.

The question now was, *Who's the real Liam Colborn?*

That question bothered me for the entire ride south. As I used Liam as my shield from the wind and rested my cheek against his back, I squeezed around his middle and tried to picture the Liam the world knew, the man who attended fancy dinners and dressed in tailored suits and styled his hair. My heart squeezed at the remote possibility that I was getting the phony version of him, that when he returned to London, he would continue to live the life he'd known before he'd escaped the camera's eye.

I didn't know where Liam was taking me, but I realized after the first few minutes of our ride that I didn't really care. Whatever version of Liam I had my arms around was the version I wanted to keep in my mind. And while he was still here, it was the only version of him I wanted to think about.

We cruised south on I-95 for forty minutes until we reached North Kingstown and continued east to Aquidneck Island. Twenty minutes later, we reached Newport, a destination I'd always heard my friends rave about but I hadn't visited until then. It was an area known for sailing and historic mansions that lined the coast.

We continued to cruise south a little more until we reached the end of Ocean Drive, where a beautiful white Victorian building sat overlooking the coast. Liam parked in the lot and gave me a sheepish grin over his shoulder. "There's somewhere I want to take you, but we need to get our keys first."

I let out a laugh, caught off guard but still exhilarated from the ride. "A room? Liam, you didn't say anything about spending the night."

His sheepish grin said it all. "I might have booked us a room." Then his eyes widened, and his grin faded slightly. "But we can turn around and go home tonight if you'd rather. I figured it would be a long ride, and…"

His voice trailed off as I looked out over the coastline at the twinkling lights of boats sailing slowly in the peninsula. Island music played from the inn as lively voices chatted and gentle waves rolled in, crashing against the rocks. It was all the perfect soundtrack to a romantic night, but I couldn't let myself believe that was what Liam had in store for us. My heart would never forgive me for it.

"No," I finally said, daring a glance back at Liam. "We should stay."

Something in his smile that followed was neither sheepish nor cocky. It was a look of relief, like he'd been banking on my response. I didn't know why, but I had a feeling I would find out soon.

We got off the bike, and he took my hand, leading me to the front desk where the woman greeted us with drinks and two keys. Our room was lofty in size with a high ceiling, white wood-paneled walls, and a wall of windows with a French door that opened out onto a balcony. But Liam didn't give me time to explore the room long. He set down a duffel bag I hadn't even seen him carrying and pulled me straight back out of the room. "C'mon."

Back downstairs, we crossed the dining area and wrap-around porch where a live band played under strung-up white lights. Then he took me down a well-lit path, over rocks and sand, between tall grass, and onto an obscure path with dimmer lights.

"Where are you taking me?" I laughed.

For someone who lived across the pond, he sure seemed familiar with this area. I hid my curiosity as I held on tightly to Liam while he pulled me over rocky terrain until we left the path to where a lighthouse stood at the bottom of a set of stairs. I gasped. "Whoa. How did you know this was here?"

Liam beamed proudly as he extended an arm to the large structure at the edge of the cliff. It wasn't tall and towering over us as I'd expect of a lighthouse, but it was still dominant in structure, with its rotating light calling attention to the jutting coastline.

"My family and I came here every year when I was little. It was Blake's favorite place in the whole world."

A fluttering erupted in my chest when I realized he'd brought me all the way here to revisit one of his childhood memories. He easily could have come alone. Liam didn't strike me as the type of person who needed the company, but for whatever reason, he'd wanted me there, and I was glad I'd come.

He led me off the path and onto a set of large rocks, where he sat and helped me down.

"My brother was obsessed with boats and used to love watching them sail by at all hours of the day. I always thought he'd move here when he got older, maybe when he retired, or maybe before that. Maybe he's here now."

My throat tightened, and I reached for Liam's hand. He was silent for a while longer, and I could sense something weighing heavy on his mind, so I waited.

Then he looked up, his eyes bloodshot, and he sucked in a deep breath. "Truth is, I didn't want to come back here alone, especially not today."

When he looked at me, a sad smile on his face, my heart tightened in my chest. "Why not today?"

"It's the anniversary of his death. I can't believe it's been seventeen years."

For a second, I couldn't breathe. Hearing him talk about his late brother was hard enough, but for him to bring me here on the anniversary of his death, I didn't know how to take that or what to say. A flood of emotions washed over me, and I really didn't know how to make sense of anything. All I could do was inch closer to him and squeeze his hand.

"Well, then I'm glad you brought me."

"You are?" He let out a laugh, his eyes still rimmed with red. "When I tried to get you to hang out with me the other night, I was just going to take you to this arcade I'd heard about. I was planning to get you embarrassingly drunk and drag you into a karaoke booth and make you sing Journey songs with me. When you wanted to wait a couple of days…"

He shrugged instead of finishing his sentence, and I realized it was all meant to be just as it had turned out.

"You know," Liam started quietly. "Even though this is hard, I haven't felt this right in quite a while." He put a fist to his heart and knocked on it before flattening it against his chest. "No one tells you what to do when someone you love dies. It's almost as if everyone expects you to grieve then just carry on with it, but this feeling." He rubbed his chest again, shaking his head. "The loss. The emptiness. It's an aching void that doesn't ever fucking go away."

Looping my arm around Liam's, I scooted closer to him, holding him tightly to me while he rested his head on mine. I didn't know what to say. Everything that came to mind felt insignificant compared to what he must have felt at that moment. So, I continued to hold onto him, just wanting Liam to know I was there. And I would continue to be there for as long as he let me.

27

LIAM

C helsea and I took showers separately when we got back to our room. She had to call her parents, so I went first, then she slipped in after me. While I debated climbing in there again, this time with her, a better idea popped into my head.

As Chelsea stepped out of the bathroom in her fluffy white bathrobe, her hair still wet from the shower, her gaze immediately fell to the tray of fresh strawberries, cheesecake, and champagne sitting on the bed. I handed her a bubbly glass, and she accepted it with a surprised smile.

"What is this?"

I leaned in and placed a kiss on her cheek, instantly getting a whiff of her sweet after-shower fragrance. "For you." I pulled back, hooking my pointer finger through the belt loop of her robe. "I know it's late, but I wanted to thank you for handling my little surprise like a champ."

Her eyes batted down to the champagne in her hand then back up to me. "You don't have to thank me, Liam. I'm glad you brought me. But…" She let the word linger as she stole a look at the cheesecake. "I definitely won't let that cheesecake go to waste."

I pulled her down onto the bed while I grabbed a forkful of dessert. Placing it against her lips, I watched her mouth part as her long lashes fluttered down so it looked like they were resting on her cheeks. "Oh my God, that's heaven," she moaned in the midst of her mouth being full.

Chuckling, I put the fork down and took a long pull of my champagne, trying to drown my oncoming excitement. We still had a bottle of champagne to go through and a tray filled with dessert. It was too soon to start feeling randy.

When Chelsea took my still half-full glass from me and climbed onto my lap, my proper intentions started to fizzle out. Her robe was parted enough for me to see her bare legs wrapped around my robed hips. Then she reached to the side to grab the fork and scooped up another piece of cream cheese.

"You have to try this." She placed the forkful against my lips, forcing me to open my mouth.

When the food hit my tongue and I started to swallow, my moan matched hers. She took turns, feeding herself then me until the entire cake was gone.

She set down the fork and made a face. "Oops. We ate it all."

I threw back my head and laughed at her play of innocence. If I hadn't known better, I just might have believed her. But Chelsea, I was learning, had quite the appetite for dessert —something I should have found out during our five-course meal the other night, but after the fourth course, we'd just repeated courses one through four over and over again.

She handed my glass of champagne back to me, and we

both took sips, our eyes locked and connected while the alcohol slipped down our throats and burned through our veins. I wanted so badly to kiss the woman who playfully swiped at her lips when she finished her glass. But for the first time ever, in the presence of a female I liked, I didn't know what to do. I worried about making the wrong move, saying the wrong thing, pushing too hard. Ultimately, I worried that if I slipped up, Chelsea would want to end things, like she'd mentioned the other day. I didn't know how this thing between us would play out, or what the wrong thing was versus the right, but I knew with every fiber of my body that I didn't want it to end.

Chelsea tilted her head and smiled back at me with half-drawn eyes. "Why are you looking at me like that?"

Setting my glass on the tray beside us, I turned back to her with a shake of my head. "I don't think I should tell you."

Her hand moved to my cheek and ran against the bristles of the facial hair I'd trimmed to a perfect scruff that morning in anticipation of tonight. My heart was batting away in my chest. "Oh, I think you should."

I wrapped an arm around her waist, keeping her locked to me as I shook my head again. "Maybe it's your turn to tell me your thoughts."

Chelsea moved her hand down to my chest, spreading my robe as she went. "How about I show you?"

I swallowed, bracing myself as she undid the fabric rope knotted at my waist. "I promise to pay very close attention."

When her hand wrapped around my thick shaft, I bit my bottom lip, muffling my guttural reaction to her touch. There was nothing better than Chelsea's small but strong hands gripping me like I was her personal plaything, there to stroke, squeeze, jerk, and fuck however she pleased.

Her smile was infectious as she leaned down and kissed me, her firm lips soft and wet as they trapped mine. Meanwhile, her movements quickened down below.

I was just starting to get used to her rhythm when she released me, pulled her robe open below, and centered herself over my cock. I watched her with so much pleasure as she sank down around me, shuddering at my base.

"Fuck me," I cursed against her lips.

Something about Chelsea Banks made me completely lose my mind when I was buried inside her, like I was a Lost Boy flying through Neverland for the very first time, and her pussy was the fairy dust that made me believe.

"That's the plan," Chelsea responded coyly as she latched onto my shoulders and picked up her speed.

And off she went, bucking over me like she was racing for the finish line. To where, I had no clue, but I wasn't about to stop and ask. I undid the knot that kept her robe pulled together on top then yanked it apart, freeing her breasts and attacking one with my tongue, then my mouth. I sucked her until she cried out, warning me of her oncoming release.

I flipped her onto her back, shoving the material of her robe out of the way then entering her again. Picking up her hips, I deepened my thrusts, trying to steady my pace to make sure she was right there with me. The second she squeezed around me was all the signal I needed to let go.

"This is exactly why I wanted to be careful with you," Chelsea said through her heavy breathing.

I lowered myself around her, propping myself up by my elbows and kissing her softly on the lips. "Why's that?"

She touched my lips, her eyes searching mine. "You're an addiction, Liam Colborn. One I can't afford to get hooked on."

I ran my lips against her collarbone and worked my way up her neck to her mouth. When I pulled away, I looked deep into her eyes. "Well, that's going to be a problem. Because I'm already hooked on you, Chelsea Banks, and whatever this is between us—I won't make it easy for you to quit."

28

CHELSEA

Every day that went by wound my chest up a little bit tighter. Three weeks had officially gone by since Liam had arrived at the Hogues' manor, marking one week left in his original plan to stay. He hadn't mentioned his plans to leave, and I hadn't asked him—mostly out of fear of knowing the answer.

However, the last weekend in Newport had definitely changed things for us—when we'd thrown all caution to the wind and stopped questioning the rights and wrongs of our relationship. Well, we'd stopped questioning it *out loud*. In my heart and head, my anxiety about the unknown was brewing like an approaching storm. I knew its wrath was coming, and I'd done a shitty job of preparing for the destruction.

I'd already attempted to board up the windows to my heart, but as soon as they'd been nailed shut, Liam had come along and busted right through them. To be fair, it hadn't taken much. I was weak in his cyclone, only finding peace in the eye of the storm. Luckily, I was smart enough to know it couldn't last forever. That had to give me some sort of advantage over the situation.

All I could ask myself was, *What's next?*

During the days and evenings following our little getaway, the twins were the perfect distraction to keep my thoughts and eyes off Liam—until my off-hours, when he would find a way to sneak me off to breakfast or dinner on his bike, depending on my schedule. Somehow, he always knew exactly when it was.

It also meant my writing time was zilch. My editor had returned her notes, and they had been haunting me, causing guilt to settle in whenever I chose to spend my free time with Liam.

"Dinner tonight," Liam whispered to me in the threshold of the twins' bedroom. "There's a place downtown I'd like to try."

"I should get some writing time in," I told him with a frown. I hated having to reject him, but I also couldn't get too far behind on my goals.

He pouted his lips, showing his disappointment, then he nodded. "Okay, then let's go somewhere right now."

"What?" I laughed at his ridiculous suggestion. "I'm watching the girls. I can't go anywhere."

He made a face. "Sure you can. Let's take a walk, go to the park, stop for lunch somewhere in the village. The girls could use some fresh air." He turned to Elizabeth and Eleanor who were gazing up at us with wide, interested eyes. "What do you think, girls? Want to go for a walk to the park?"

They jumped up with excitement, dropping their dolls, one whose hair was now tangled in a hairbrush Eleanor had been using.

I sighed and turned to Liam with a gentle laugh. "Fine,

but you get to pull Brendan off the phone. He's been talking to some girl for the past hour."

Liam chuckled before turning. "On it."

Minutes later, we were heading down Blackstone Boulevard with Elizabeth on Liam's shoulders and Eleanor on Brendan's. At the park, we played chase and helped the girls down the slides until everyone was out of breath.

It was Liam's idea to walk a little farther to Spill the Tea. Apparently, he hadn't shown his face in there since he'd seen himself on television, but he was in need of a tea fix, so I agreed. The girls didn't argue a bit. They knew if they went to visit my parents, they would leave on a sugar high we would all regret later. So we went.

Dread sank into my gut when we walked up to the tearoom and I spotted Gwen sitting at a round table outside with a small group of her friends. They had already seen us approaching and were waving before we could do anything about it. Not that I would have made everyone turn around, but I would have been lying if I didn't admit that I hoped to avoid the woman every time I paid my parents a visit.

"Chelsea," Gwen said, clapping her hands together like we were old friends.

"Happy to see she's kept up with the accent," Liam muttered to me, making me stifle a laugh.

"It's been ages." Gwen's friendly eyes had moved to the twins, but now they were on Liam, her lids shooting wide in surprise. "Oh my."

Ignoring the woman's reaction, I pushed the door open. "Has it been ages?" I smiled and placed my hands on the girls' backs to keep them moving.

"Wait, dear. Aren't you going to introduce me to your new friend?"

I pinched out a smile and darted a look at Liam. "Oh, of

course. Forgive me. Gwen, I'd like to introduce you to my friend Liam. Liam, this is Gwen, a regular here at Spill the Tea."

"You don't say," Liam said, his charming smile as perfect as could be. "It's a pleasure to meet your acquaintance, Gwen."

I stifled a laugh at his exaggerated British accent.

Gwen's mouth fell open at the sound of him speaking. "Oh, you're British. How on earth did you and Chelsea meet?"

I jumped in, not wanting Liam to say more than he should, for his benefit and mine. "He's just visiting the Hogues from London, Gwen. Don't get too excited." I smiled at Liam, hoping he understood my explanation to the woman.

"Very well," she said, giving us both a suspicious glance, then her eyes widened again. "Wait. Did you say your name is Liam?" A smile blossomed on her face. "As in William?"

I looked at Liam, twisting my brows in confusion. But a second later, I made the connection before she even said a word. *Oh, shit. No.*

Gwen clapped her hands together with glee. "As in—"

Don't say it. Don't say it. Don't say it.

"Willy?"

I. Was. Mortified. My entire body felt as if I'd just walked straight through an inferno. Thank God Brendan and the girls had zero idea what Gwen was talking about.

"Well," I said, rushing the girls along. "I hope you've been well, Gwen. We better get inside. It was nice seeing you again."

With that, I shoved everyone inside the tearoom and let the kids run behind the counter to greet my mom. Liam chuckled beside me while Brendan followed the kids but stayed in front of the counter.

I sighed and turned to Liam. "Is it normal to feel so anxious over a woman you hardly know? She's just so nosy."

Liam shrugged. "She strikes me as a lonely woman who lives vicariously through others. She's a fan of yours, I'd say."

I laughed. "A fan of my sex life."

"With all those giant willies you manage, I can see why." He winked and wrapped an arm over my shoulders. Leaning in, he pressed a kiss to my cheek. "Don't worry, love. I know mine is your favorite."

Mortified, I jabbed Liam in the side with my elbow, causing him to wince while laughing way too hard at his own joke. I joined Brendan at the counter, smiling at my mom, who had one twin in each arm as she let them pick treats from the glass display case. When she finally set the girls down, they each had a cookie in their hands, and she looked up at the rest of us. That was when she saw Liam coming up behind me.

I hadn't thought much about my mother's reaction to seeing me with Liam, but I had expected her to be shocked—then have lots and lots of questions.

"Well, hello there," she greeted him with a curious twinkle in her eyes. "You're back for another tea?" Then she looked between the lot of us and twisted her lips at me.

My pulse raced through my veins and my heart hammered away in my chest as I waited for the first question to strike.

"Sweetie," she started, "do you mind giving this gentleman some room?" Then she smiled politely at him.

"Um." Liam darted a panicked look between me and my mom. "That's quite all right. She's no bother."

Brendan nudged my side and leaned over to me. "Are you going to tell her, or should I?"

Biting back my laugh, I gestured with my hands for him to do the honors.

"Actually, Mrs. Banks, this is Liam—a friend of my dad's. Liam's been staying with us for the past few weeks."

"Oh," my mom said, her eyes shooting wide in surprise then fading into whatever connection she was making. Her gaze shifted between Liam's and mine. "So, then you two know each other."

I nodded, suddenly wondering if I should have told her about Liam sooner. I definitely wouldn't mention all the times she'd seen him on the television but hadn't put two and two together. I imagined that one day I would tell her the funny story about the British Bachelor who'd often visited her tearoom when she was none the wiser, but for now, I was happy for the secrecy.

"That's right," I said. "Liam's on holiday from London."

"Is that so?" she asked him. "When do you have to return?"

There was an awkward silence that settled between us, namely Liam and me. I swallowed. He darted a look at me, but I didn't dare turn to meet his gaze. I didn't want to pressure him to respond, partly because I didn't want him to respond at all—not until we'd had a chance to talk just the two of us.

"Soon, I'm afraid."

Liam's words were all the makings of a whirlpool, sending my heart into a spiral to the pit of my stomach.

"But I quite like the area," Liam continued. "I'll have to plan another visit once I take care of some things back home. Maybe Chelsea will be my tour guide again."

I heard his follow-up and smiled, but my heart didn't take the bait. It was far too deep, weighted with swirling debris of my thoughts.

"I'm sure she would love that," my mom gushed. She looked genuinely pleased by his words, and it was then that I noticed her eyes were bright and shining. I knew that look of hope—hope that her daughter had finally found "the one" to settle down and make her grandbabies with, hope that just made the inevitable so much worse.

Liam was leaving. Soon. And I had no guarantees that I would ever see him again.

My heart had been aching all afternoon and into the evening after I left the twins to head home. How could I become so attached to a guy after three weeks? I was being ridiculous. I couldn't even look at Liam after we left the tearoom for fear of bursting into tears or asking him what he meant by "soon."

When was soon? In a day, in a week? A month? All of it was too soon, and it was my own damn fault for letting myself get in too deep. Hadn't that been precisely what I'd been trying to avoid before succumbing to his spell?

The trouble was, I knew exactly what the breaking point had been for me. It was when he'd taken me to Newport and confided in me about his brother, when I'd felt the vulnerability wrapped around his words. I didn't just have a crush on Liam. I wanted more of him just like that, vulnerable, raw, nothing like what I'd seen on that reality show.

I may not have wanted to believe it straight away, but Liam wasn't the guy the media had painted him to be, and I was totally fucked.

I'd just thrown on some cotton shorts and a tank top when the knock came at the side door of the pool house. It was the first night in the past week that I hadn't left it open for him to just walk right in. We'd gotten too comfortable, and I knew we had to change that. But also, I hadn't been expecting him so soon, not when Simon and Bridget were home next door and everyone was still awake.

Glancing at the time, I confirmed it was only eight thirty, way too early for Liam to come by. By the time I pulled open the door a few seconds later, my head was spinning with all the reasons why he would show up unexpectedly. But all thoughts vanished when I got an eyeful of him outside my door.

He was wearing his favorite sweatpants that he'd labeled "easy access," and that was all. His chest was bare, and his hair was wet like he'd just gotten out of the shower. My first thought was to step into his arms and run my hands through his thick locks. My second thought was that he'd just left my bosses' house looking *like that*.

"What are you doing here?" I hissed as I glanced over his shoulder like someone could be following him. But the entire section surrounding the pool area was closed off with tall shrubs and a gate. No one was there. No one could see us.

Liam chuckled and stepped inside, kicking the door shut behind him. Then he placed his hands on my hips and pushed me backward as he moved us into my bedroom. "Visiting my girl, of course."

My eyes widened, and I shook my head, flattening my palms on his chest. "But Simon and Bridget could have seen you come here. You usually wait until they're asleep," I scolded.

He was still all grins as he picked me up and wrapped my legs around his waist. "I told Simon I had to go on a run."

It was hard not to laugh at the ridiculous lie. Liam was a swimmer and as athletic as they come, but I'd never seen him run. "Wearing that?"

He shrugged. "Why not?"

I shook my head and rolled my eyes. I couldn't even look

at him. "They still could have been watching you, Liam. The entrance to the pool is a little bit off your pretend jogging trail."

"Simon and Bridget were playing with the twins in the master bedroom. They didn't see me." Then his lids narrowed. "But I probably shouldn't return until I've worked up a sweat." His mouth dipped lower until he was at my neck, kissing and sucking while his hands made their way under my shirt. "I missed you."

Those words. So simple, so sweet. At least they should have been. The problem wasn't that he had said them but that I missed him too. The reality behind that sentiment was the scariest of all. Because it had only been a few hours since I'd last seen him. What would happen when he was thousands of miles away with a five-hour time difference? Just asking myself some basic questions tied my insides in knots.

He was running his kisses along my jawline when I swallowed and dared to bring up my fears. "We should talk, Liam."

His kisses slowed, and I swore I heard him sigh. "Not tonight, okay?"

His gentle eyes met mine for a few moments before I gave in and nodded. "Okay."

But as his fingers brushed over my breasts, searching, teasing, I couldn't help but notice something different in his touch, something possessive yet raw, like he was trying to slow down the clock by taking his time with me.

When he set me back on my feet, it was only to give himself enough time to undress us before I was back in his arms. My arms wrapped tightly around his neck as he pushed into me, his pace excruciatingly slow. His kisses were tortuously sweet, his breath hot like fire as it came in waves over my skin.

Deep down, I knew what Liam was doing to me that night, and just like all the nights that had come before it, I allowed it. I let him claim me with his touch. But that was the first night I knew with every fiber in my being that Liam Colborn was worse than a tattoo inked permanently on my skin. Liam was a branding iron permanently etching himself into my heart.

29

LIAM

By the time I crept in through the back door of the Hogues' house, it was well past midnight. I was returning with a heavier heart than I'd left with. After her mother's question at the tearoom earlier today, all I knew was that I wanted to see her, hold her, kiss her, touch her. I wanted Chelsea in all the ways I'd come to familiarize myself with. Most of all, I wanted clarity.

Heading back to London had always been the plan, but the question of when was still unclear. All I knew was that if Chelsea and I were to pursue something more than what we'd established, then I would need to shut the door on my past once and for all.

I shut the back door quietly behind me and turned. My heart punched through my chest when I saw Simon standing there with fury written all over his face. "I thought I'd made myself clear."

There was no point in darting around the truth or trying to hide from it any longer, especially knowing the end was near. "Shit, Simon. You scared the bloody hell out of me."

"I had my suspicions, but I was hoping for the best. I still am." He raised his brows and pointed to the seat beside him. "Sit and start talking."

Sighing, I did as he said, but I didn't need more prodding to confess. It was time to get everything out in the open, and I would start with Simon. I told him *almost* everything. Leaving the intimate details aside, I was honest with him about how Chelsea and I had met, about how I'd gotten to know her so fast, and how I'd fallen so deeply. We talked about Blake and the trip Chelsea and I had taken to Newport. We talked about an uncertain future and all that it entailed.

In the end, Simon wasn't angry. At least—not for the same reasons he'd started to be angry. It seemed, in some strange way, he understood. "So, this isn't some kind of fling then?"

I shook my head, looking him dead in the eye. "Not at all, Simon. You have my word. I care about Chelsea quite a lot."

Simon chuckled and shook his head. "Well, mate. Sounds like you've gotten yourself into a predicament."

"It will be fine. I'm handling it."

He raised his brows. "Are you? Have you both forgotten where you live? Why you're here?"

I fought my frustration and took in a deep breath, then exhaled slowly. "No one has forgotten anything."

"What happens next, Liam? Have you thought about that?"

The plan had always been to return to London when I had a clear head so I could deal with the wrath of my decisions. Now, I wasn't so sure that was the best idea. "Not really, no. But I know I need to figure it out."

"Well, for starters, you can turn on your phone."

Simon pushed a silver object across the island, and I caught it before it fell over the edge. It was my phone. I hadn't even looked at the thing the entire three weeks of my visit.

"I charged it for you."

I couldn't for the life of me figure out why Simon would have dug around for my phone and charged it for me. That felt a little out of character. "But why—"

"Bart is why." Simon rolled his eyes and tapped his phone on the counter. "He rang a few hours ago. I went looking for you and realized you never came back from your run. That's when I put two and two together."

"Hold up. Bart rang you? But—"

"He threatened to leak your whereabouts to the media if you didn't call him back."

That daft bastard. "How did he find out I was here?"

Simon ran a hand through his hair and blew out a breath. "Not for me to worry about. However, my family is something you should worry about. I let you stay, Liam, but I can't have my family dragged into your mess. You need to go back to London, and you need to fix this."

"I will," I promised. The last thing I wanted was for Simon and his family to get dragged into my mess in any way. "I'll call Bart back and see what I need to do. You don't need to worry." I hopped off the stool, clutched my phone in my hand, and jogged downstairs to my room, where I called Bart.

"It's about bloody time, you daft twat." Bart's greeting was about as cool and unpleasant as I'd expect.

"You rang?"

What proceeded was a string of curse words and British slang that not even I could comprehend, followed by a growled "Get home now!"

I threw myself backward onto my bed and squeezed my eyes shut. "I need more time."

"Time? Time?" Bart's voice continued to rise. "Three weeks, Liam. You disappeared weeks ago, and you want more time?"

"How did you even know I was here?"

Bart chuckled. "Do you think you're Batman? You think a man like you can waltz into a British tearoom wearing shades and go completely undetected? Are you mad? Everyone has been stalking your hashtags, Liam. Me included."

I sat up again, not believing it was true. If someone had recognized me, surely they would have said something. "What?" I asked while reactivating one of my social media accounts and typing in my hashtag.

"Once I knew you were in Providence, I rang your mum. She wants you to come home too. If you think she's been free and clear of the media just because you skipped town, then you're wrong. She's been hounded."

My heart sank at the thought of my parents being swarmed with people wanting information. Then I saw what Bart was referencing on social media. "Holy fuck."

#LiamColborn #BritishBachelor #Spotted #Providence. The string of clever hashtags seemed never-ending after a single photo of me stepping outside of Spill the Tea was shared thousands of times.

"Holy fuck, yes. Come home, Liam. We still have time to salvage this. To my understanding, the Hogues want nothing to do with you and your fame. Come home before the others figure out where you're staying too."

"You're leaving?"

After I got off the phone with Bart, I went straight back to Chelsea's and told her everything. Then, with tears glistening in her eyes, we made love. We were currently wrapped in each other's arms, our heavy breaths finally evening out. She lay at my side as I stared up at the ceiling, watching the orange reflection of the flickering candle at her bedside.

When I'd lied to Simon and Bridget about going on a run earlier in the night, I'd known we needed to talk about me leaving. But after seeing her, I'd shoved it all aside for a chance to be with her without worries, without that looming cloud that had been hanging over us since the very beginning, thickening by the day, only promising more destruction when it finally was unleashed. Now, it was too late to run for cover. The storm was upon us.

While I'd stayed away from the world I'd left behind, it hadn't erased what would be waiting for me when I finally returned. And while I would choose to ignore my past forever to make a new life here, that wasn't the way the world worked. There needed to be closure, and I needed to be the one who sought it out.

"I wish I didn't have to go. Everything I walked away from is still waiting there for me. There's just no delaying it anymore, not now that they know where I am."

"We always knew this was coming."

I hated the way her sad eyes stared back into mine, like I was crushing her when I couldn't think of a single other solution. When she didn't say another word, an idea sprang to mind.

"You could come with me—for a week, for forever." I smiled to show her there was some levity in my serious words. Even in my own head, I knew the suggestion wasn't my best idea. But what was the alternative? Leaving Providence and not knowing if or when I would see Chelsea again? That option felt incomprehensible.

Creases formed in her brows while her eyes searched mine. "Come with you to London?"

I nodded and swallowed, knowing how selfish my question

sounded, but I couldn't stop my mind from spinning solutions on how we could make it work. *We'd find a flat for the two of us. She'd meet my family. She'd write while I dealt with the press.* I could almost imagine a happy life.

"Oh, Liam."

Her face looked completely crestfallen, and I readied myself for the rejection I should have expected the second the words came out of my mouth. My question had been unfair for so many reasons, namely the Hogues.

She shifted, propping herself up so she was looking down on me. "I love my life here. My parents are here. My friends are here. I'm about to publish my first book. I can't uproot myself now."

My gut churned as I felt my control over the situation, what little I ever had of it, slipping through my fingers. "Maybe you could plan a visit soon. You'd love London." I felt the stretch of my words. Our situation was far too complicated to create a happy solution from it.

"Then what?" Chelsea's shaky voice sharpened my focus on her. "I come visit for a week and then what? Then you come back here for a visit, and we rotate once a month?"

I opened my mouth, more than willing to agree to that idea, but then I saw her incredulous expression—the one that told me she'd given up on us before we'd even gotten started—and snapped it back shut.

She sat up quickly, the sheet falling away from her breasts as she pulled her hair up into a quick ponytail. I swallowed and ran my fingers up her spine, wanting to calm her before things got too heated. We needed a solution, not more chaos.

"We'll figure it out."

She looked at me over her shoulder. "I can't see how."

I sat up, feeling a charge of desperation run through my veins. I pressed my lips to her back and inhaled her sweet scent—a calming breath before speaking again. "Maybe that's the beauty in all of this. We can't see how it will all play out, but that doesn't mean it won't or can't or shouldn't. It just means that part of our story hasn't been written yet."

She studied me for a minute before a small smile broke loose on her beautiful face. "I hate to break this to you, Liam, but most readers hate cliff-hangers."

I thought about that statement and how all I'd been doing for the past few months was reacting to what everyone else thought of me, strangers, women who never truly knew or loved me. What a waste that was, caring for people who knew nothing about what was good for me.

My eyes held Chelsea's, and I cupped her cheek as my mouth met her ear. I wanted her to hear my words with every ounce of feeling they were backed with. "Then it's a good thing we're writing this story for us and not the whole damn world."

30

CHELSEA

The day before Liam was scheduled to leave town, summer turned to fall. It was only a week after our talk in my bedroom, but I considered it a sign—that even though the seasons were changing, Liam and I would hold strong, like a tree that adapted with the changing climate. That was what we would do, and we would be stronger for it in the end.

I soaked in his optimistic words, his promise to return, battling the doubtful thoughts that shot up like weeds when I least expected them. I wanted to believe that we could continue dating after he dealt with things back home. After falling so deeply, I needed to believe that was true.

I used to be one of those people who had a plan for everything. Even the things I didn't want to do made it into my planner so the job would get tackled and there would be no question of my future. But at some point along the way, I realized that my obsession with planning had played into my blindness of where I was in life versus where I truly wanted to be.

Letting go had changed my perspective in so many ways, and I hoped it would keep me afloat now.

We were hanging out in the park on Blackstone Boulevard, which we'd arrived at after much debate. Before today, we'd been keeping to ourselves in my poolhouse, but we were both going stir-crazy. As soon as we arrived, Liam spotted a shaved-ice truck and bought us one to share while I lay out a blanket for us to sit on.

I sat between his legs as he fed us both spoonfuls as we chatted. It was simple, fun, and I loved that we didn't have to sneak around behind Bridget and Simon's backs anymore. We'd even all had dinner together last night, like one big happy family, and Liam didn't hide where he spent his nights anymore. It all felt so natural, so real, so right.

"What's the first thing you're going to do when you get back home?"

"Think of you."

His quick answer made me smile. I turned to glare at him teasingly. He chuckled and kissed my cheek.

"I'm serious, Liam. I want to know."

"Okay, okay. I haven't made any plans. No point, really. Bart warned me that we'll be busy from the moment I hit the tarmac."

I frowned, my feelings for this Bart guy becoming over-whelmingly negative. Bart was Liam's producer, one who had specifically been assigned to him during his time on *British Bachelor*. I'd yet to hear a single story that made me believe he had Liam's best interests at heart.

A shrill ring sounded, and I groaned at yet another phone call Liam had to take.

"Speak of the Devil," Liam muttered while reading the caller ID.

"Bart?"

He nodded. "I'll tell him I'll call him back."

"You don't have to. It might be important."

"Okay, well, I'll make it quick." He tapped his phone to answer the call and put it to his ear. "Hiya, Bart."

Ever since Liam had turned his phone back on, it hadn't stopped going off. Mostly, it was Bart making plans and informing him of conversations he would be having with producers in preparation for Liam's return. Sometimes it was a producer who was trying to cut through Bart and speak directly to Liam. Every so often I would hear him pick up the phone and answer with a "Hiya, Mum" in a soft voice that melted my heart.

The second Liam answered the phone this time, I could hear Bart's anger practically blow through the phone. I made a face at Liam in response and grabbed the cup of flavored ice from his hands. Settling into his arms, I scooped a mouthful to satisfy me while I tried to focus on the people in the park rather than what Liam's conversation was about.

The park's paths were fairly crowded, considering it was the weekend. A family of four strolled by while the kids played tag in the grass. A boy with a dog walked him on a leash. A group of bicyclists, a man snapping photos with a large black lens, a girl riding her yellow skateboard to the ramps nearby— at a quick glance, it seemed like the perfect day. There wasn't a cloud in the sky. The birds were chirping, and Liam was holding me tightly, but I couldn't shake the feeling that something was off.

My eyes darted around again, seeing all the same things I'd spotted before. I let out a heavy breath to try to shake my nerves. Ever since that photo of Liam had appeared on social media, I'd done some investigating of my own. That photo had been taken on the day we'd visited Spill the Tea with the kids. Liam hadn't had his shades on, and the photo had been taken by someone right outside the shop. After a quick search through all the shared photos, I'd found the original post.

Gwen had taken that photo. At some point during our visit, she'd made the connection and taken her gossip to a whole new level by making it public. Luckily, she'd left the kids and me out of the photo. I couldn't even imagine Simon and Bridget's fury if the twins and Brendan had been plastered all over social media too.

To top everything off, my mom had called me the day after the photos leaked, questioning me about Liam. I was vague but promised to tell her everything later. The less she knew while cameras started to pop up at the tearoom was safer for all.

Liam hung up from his call and grabbed for what was left of the shaved ice. "You sneaky woman," he growled, making me laugh.

"It was melting," I said in my defense.

He growled again, this time burying his mouth in my neck, and a wave of shivers erupted over my skin.

In all the chaos, one thing that remained was the calm that fell upon Liam when he would hang up the phone, every single time.

"How do you do that?"

"Do what?" He took the last bite and set down the empty cup beside us.

"Return to this playful, calm person after you've been spoken to like that. It's not normal for people to yell all the time."

Liam chuckled and wrapped his arms around my waist. "Bart wasn't yelling. That's just how he talks. But to answer your question, I'm only calm because I'm here with you."

I looked back at him and smiled. "That's sweet."

He leaned in, touching his nose to mine. "It's true, which

means I'll be a neurotic mess when I leave tomorrow. Are you sure you can't come with me? I need you to save me from imploding, Chelsea."

My heart beat so hard it felt like it was enveloping me in its rhythm. Instead of responding with an answer I knew would disappoint us both, I pressed my lips to his and sighed. We sat like that for a long time, slow-kissing and avoiding goodbye until daylight started to fade away.

He threaded his fingers through mine and moved his mouth to my ear. "Remember the night we met?"

I instantly laughed at the memory of the terror that had come over me when his loud music and splashing in the pool had woken me up. "I could never forget. I was terrified."

He chuckled. "Not for long."

I met his eyes over my shoulder. "I don't know if I've ever stopped being terrified of you. Only now it's for other reasons."

He nodded, and our silence spoke enough for us. He felt the same. Then his mouth moved to my lips, and he spoke against them. "How about one more swim before I have to leave tomorrow?"

My insides squeezed at the question. We were down to counting the hours before his departure, and the aches I was starting to feel were a preview of what I was sure would come. "Okay," I whispered back.

We gathered our things, made our way back home, then separated to change into our swimsuits. I chose a white two-piece he'd yet to see me in, fully intending to leave him with an image he would never forget.

Liam was already swimming laps when I sat down at the edge of the pool and sank my feet in the water. I watched his perfect strokes, the way his muscles rippled beneath his skin, and the way the water moved for him like he was the conductor to its flow.

After taking his last lap, he popped up between my legs and grinned. "You're going to be a hard one to leave tomorrow, Chelsea Banks."

Leaning down, I met his mouth with mine and kissed him while running my hands through his hair. He lifted me off the edge then pulled me into the water. When my legs wrapped around his waist, he sighed into my neck, making my whole body erupt with goose bumps.

"I'm going to miss this," he whispered.

I swallowed around the lump in my throat while my eyes burned with oncoming tears. Tightening my hold, I placed my lips at his ear. "Well, then you better hurry back to me, Liam Colborn."

He pulled back slightly, his lips twisting into a smile. "As fast as I can."

31

LIAM

After an entire night of lying awake with Chelsea, I spent the long flight to London sleeping. I was still in a daze when I exited the plane and found Bart waiting for me outside of customs. With a stern look, he nodded in greeting and clapped me on the back.

"Well, it's about bloody time, mate. You've got the press up in arms awaiting your arrival. I hope you're not too knackered."

Speaking of the press. I looked around, confused as to why the car we were heading toward wasn't flooded with those annoying bastards and their cameras. "Awaiting my arrival, eh?"

Bart looked around and grinned. "I told 'em you were already at an undisclosed hotel in Kensington. The nutters are camped out around town, thanks to your cock-up." Then he jabbed his finger toward the open car door. "Now get in. We'll talk about the plan."

The dreaded plan. Bart had been working on his so-called

plan for the past week since I'd finally called him and told him I was making arrangements to come home.

"Good. We can talk about the plan on the way to my flat."

Bart shook his head while he tapped a message out on his phone. "No time." Then he nodded to a hanging garment bag that I hadn't noticed was next to me until he'd pointed it out. "Change into that. You have a meeting in an hour."

"Don't be a wanker. I just landed. I need a shower, then I need my bed."

Bart's eyes snapped to mine. "You've been gone for a month, and suddenly you want to stop for a kip? Afraid not, mate. We've got to get you out of this mess straightaway."

Bart had always been a wanker with his own agenda, but he was also the only person I remotely trusted. "Care to share your plan with me? I know nothing, yet you have me booked for a meeting in an hour. Who am I meeting with?"

"Vince wants to have a word to control the narrative of what happens next. It's only fair since you up and left without a word. You still have a chance to salvage your contract."

I huffed and leaned my head back into the seat. Just the mention of Vince made my body crawl with annoyance. Vince was the creator and executive director of *British Bachelor*. The show had been his baby for fourteen years, and he never let anyone forget that.

"I wouldn't have left if the media hadn't made a mockery of me thanks to all the bad edits I was given."

Bart was silent for a moment, which was completely unlike him, but I knew he agreed with what I was saying. "I agree you got the shit end of the stick, but what did you expect? You broke three hearts in one night, leaving us without any footage for a finale. You left us with no choice."

"I didn't break three hearts. You know that as well as I do."

"Right, but you should have let it all play out on camera instead of walking away."

"And break up with them later when they were expecting a proposal? I couldn't do that to any of them."

"Even Francesca?" Bart asked the question with as much bitterness as I felt.

Bart had been there with me, and he'd been just as surprised as I was to find out that Francesca was nothing but a media-hungry wannabe actress.

"As soon as the cameras pointed in the opposite direction, her true colors became crystal clear. She was a completely different person, but I can't call her out for any of that, now can I?"

Bart shook his head. "You most certainly cannot."

"Great. So it's me who looks like the arse. I sure felt like one too."

Bart twisted his face. "Don't tell me you were daft enough to believe the lead spot on a high-profile show like this didn't come with puppet strings."

I was silent, reveling in my own stupidity for signing on to do the show in the first place. The weight of it all was finally coming fully into picture. The last thing I wanted was to go back to a world where I was controlled by someone else's narrative. Where was the reality in that? But I couldn't even form my first syllable before Bart was speaking again.

"This is how the game works. Now you need to finish what you signed on to do."

"Or I walk away completely and end my contract. I'm no one's puppet, and it's not like I need the money."

I made the mistake of letting my gaze settle back on his. Bart's level glare blazed back at me with anger. "Oh, you don't, do ya? Well, I don't give a shit about your financial situation. When they assigned me as your producer, my arse got put on the line too. Your actions affect others. And do I also need to remind you of a contract you signed with the network? The moment you walked away from that show, you opened yourself up to one hell of a lawsuit. Vince will be more than happy than to pursue legal action if his precious ratings are at stake. You might not need the money, but you sure as hell can't afford to lose any."

Well, fuck. He had a good point. I chose not to test the waters any further and, instead, got dressed in the gray tailored suit, tossed some water on my hair, and tried to make it appear somewhat presentable. In minutes, I looked like the British Bachelor again—the man the show had created—the man I thought, at the time, I wanted to be.

Just wearing the suit made me feel as slimy as I had back then, like a fraud dressed to fool the world, and I instantly craved what I had back in Providence. Not just Chelsea, though she was my number-one reason for wanting to go back, but because, for the first time in a long time, I'd felt like myself.

This wasn't me. This was the lie I'd agreed to live, but I was willing to come back to make for the quickest and cleanest exit possible. Only then would I be able to move forward.

"Well," I said when Bart still hadn't looked up from his phone. "What's the plan?"

He sent his message and slid his phone back in his pocket. "Right. The plan." He leaned back against the seat, setting his arms on either side of him. "Our plan is to agree with everything they ask of you to avoid a breach of contract."

My jaw dropped. "That's it? That's your brilliant plan?"

Bart raised his brows in a challenge. "You'll go to whatever interviews they book for you throughout the week, ending with a live reunion taping on Monday night."

"Wait a bloody minute," I said with a shake of my head. I

must not have heard him right. "Reunion taping? They already aired that."

"Precisely. And you missed it. Lucky for you, they rebooked it, and all of your lovely ladies will be there to greet you. Directly following the taping, you have bookings on two late-night shows, then you can have your kip after everything you're scheduled for throughout the week."

"Can you be more specific?"

Bart scrolled through his phone then read off dozens of radio and television and entertainment news names. I was already overwhelmed.

"You'll be under fire this week," Bart said in close. "I hope you're ready."

I shook my head, letting out a frustrated laugh. "Why do these people act like I owe them something? This is my life, and they're making a mockery of it."

"Considering you signed up for a show where you were expected to fall in love and failed, I believe you do, in fact, owe them something. You were a coward by leaving everyone hanging. Now it's time to make the viewers happy."

As much as I wanted to lunge for Bart for calling me a coward, his words rang true deep in my chest. I *had* been a coward. Disappearing had been much easier than facing the aftermath that had surfaced once viewers saw that I couldn't commit. In the end, everyone was just doing their jobs. Unfortunately for me, I didn't get a say in what gave the network good ratings. I was just the bait.

We arrived at the network's building in Marylebone's Portland Place where we were escorted from the parking garage into the back entrance of the office then to a small conference room. When we entered, a group of executives, producers, directors—familiar faces from when we'd taped the show—were sitting in wait.

As soon as everyone spotted me, they were on their feet, wearing smiles that told me they were glad to see me again. I wasn't fooled by the warm hugs and firm handshakes or the encouraging voices telling me that they were so glad I was back. I was their puppet, nothing more, in a world they had created, and I had malfunctioned miserably.

Bart led me to a spot on the other side of the table, then we all settled into our seats as the conference door closed with a heavy boom.

"How was your holiday, Liam? Well worth it, we hope." Vince Petri, Executive Producer of *British Bachelor*, was directly across the table from me when he spoke, sending a quick chill up my spine. He was in his early fifties with smooth tan skin and white-white hair. He was a legend to the entertainment community and a man to be feared behind closed doors. Out of everyone in the room, he was the one I trusted the least.

"It was a much-needed getaway. Thank you for asking."

Bart shot me a hard look and shook his head, telling me not to respond again. "Liam is eager to make things right."

Vince leaned forward slightly while his broad shoulders pushed back. "Let me remind everyone here that Liam walked off a production set while still filming, was a no-show on the reunion episode, then skipped out on every single scheduled appearance since. I should hope he wants to make things right."

I shifted in my seat and glared at Bart beside me. "I do, Vince. You have my word on that."

Already, the conversation was going horribly wrong. I wasn't there to defend myself or to play into the media's hands. I was there to move on and to figure out how to do so.

"Well, good." Vince gave a smug smile. "I have to say, up until that final episode aired, our ratings were the highest they've ever been. We lost a lot of credibility as a show when you did what you did."

I nodded. "In retrospect, I do believe I could have handled things better. I reacted poorly to the situation, and I'm ready to discuss that. However, I can't take all the credit for the fan and media's reaction. It would have been nice if the show had given me an edit that didn't make me look like the bad guy, but—" I raised my hands in the air in a gesture to show I was ready for the consequences.

Vince's chuckle echoed off the walls. Then he threw his hands up. "Someone had to be the bad guy."

I clenched my jaw before releasing it to speak. "I didn't sign on to be your bad guy."

"You certainly weren't our hero in the end, now were you? Heroes don't disappear when everyone needs them."

Buried anger crawled out from my chest with Vince's words. I'd kept so much of my frustration toward the show tucked away to the point that even I'd started to believe the man they'd painted me to be. Sure, I could take accountability for my actions. Disappearing had been wrong. But sitting there and listening to Vince speak only reminded me of the toxic environment I'd walked away from.

"I *disappeared* because, at the time, I felt like it was the only option. I wasn't in love with those women, and they weren't in love with me. Explaining that to the media after the way I was portrayed in that final episode was impossible."

Bart rested a hand on my arm, signaling for me to refrain from speaking. He turned to Vince. "I think we're all here for the right reasons. Let's talk about the week ahead. It's my strong feeling that we need to expose Liam's vulnerability here. He thought he was ready for love, but clearly, he wasn't. I think that's a very human thing to realize."

Vince pursed his lips, and he looked to be pondering

Bart's suggestion. "Yes, but is it enough to make Liam relatable to the fans of the show again? That's what they're looking for."

Bart settled back into his chair. "Liam, you can correct me, but I believe it's deeper than anything ever discussed on the show. There was a lot of talk about your brother's death. Viewers are well aware of your tragic loss, since it was such a significant topic of conversation. You've already mentioned how it's affected many aspects of your life, especially when it comes to women. Do you believe that may have played a part in your commitment issues?"

My mouth snapped shut again, as I realized that what he was saying was true. "It absolutely played a role, but Blake isn't the reason I walked away from the women. I walked away because, if Blake's life has taught me anything, it's that life is short, and you can't live it with regrets. I could have moved forward with any of those women, but I would have been choosing them for all the wrong reasons."

Bart twisted his lips. "Right. But maybe we can word it differently. Like—" He turned to Vince, who was completely tuned into the young producer's words. "With the anniversary of Blake's death approaching, Liam was triggered, then he froze when it came to the thought of settling down."

Vince pounded a fist on the table and beamed back at Bart. "Yes. That's bloody brilliant. And true, right, Liam?"

I couldn't argue with a single thing they had said. I nodded.

Bart clapped me on the back. "The cast of women will have sympathy for Liam's situation. So will the viewers. And it continues the storyline of how Liam has never been able to settle down, but there's hope for you still because you believe that the one is out there."

At the same moment as he finished his sentence, Chelsea's

face popped into my head. The thought of settling down didn't seem like such a bad thing when I thought of her. I let out a heavy breath, finally feeling closer to the finish line than I had in a long time. Soon, the nightmare would be over.

Vince sat back and smiled. "There's only one thing we need to discuss."

The room grew quiet as Vince snapped his fingers, and his assistant jumped out of his seat and handed his boss a manila folder. Without even looking at it, he slid the folder to Bart at me.

My heart sank as I watched Vince's expectant expression focus on Bart as he opened the folder. "Oh, bloody hell."

I didn't want to look. I didn't want to even entertain the idea that something could make this situation any worse than it already was. But when Bart slid the opened folder in front of me, I didn't have a choice but to look down. *Bloody hell is right.*

The top photo was of Chelsea and me sitting on a blanket in the park. She was between my legs, and I was kissing her on her cheek. My heart caught in my chest as one by one I went through the photos to see that whoever had followed Chelsea and me to the park had caught every single private moment between us—our kisses, our shaved ice, the way I'd looked longingly into her silver-blue eyes before she'd kissed me back. God, I missed her.

Anger boiled in my chest before my eyes snapped to Vince. "You had me followed?"

"Who is this, Liam?" Bart cut in.

"Her name is Chelsea Banks," Vince said. "She's the nanny for Simon and Bridget Hogue."

"What?" Bart asked, directing his question at me. "The doctor you were staying with in Providence? Why haven't you mentioned a bloody thing about her?"

"It was no one's business. I don't want Chelsea dragged

into all of this." My eyes snapped to Vince. "Have these been made public?"

Vince shook his head. "No. These are the only photos I know about, and I don't plan to let them out of my hands." Everyone in the room gave a collective sigh of relief.

"Good. Let's keep it that way."

"Are you sure?" Vince asked, his eyes sparkling with mischief as he worked through his thoughts aloud. "Talk about a shocking twist. Viewers would eat this up. Liam walks away from the show because he doesn't believe he'll ever find love. He runs away to Providence then falls in love with a *nanny?*" He let out a boisterous laugh, his eyes wide. "The drama couldn't have been better if we'd planned it." Then he turned to address my producer. "What do you think, Bart?"

I shook my head hard, not giving Bart a chance to respond. There was no point. "No, absolutely not. Chelsea is off-limits. End of discussion."

"But—" Bart started.

I stood, cutting him off, slamming my palms on the conference table. "The answer is no. I won't consider her involvement for a moment. Do not ask me again." With a curt nod, I made my way to the exit, ending the conversation.

32

CHELSEA

The shrill of my phone ringing yanked me from a deep sleep and a very good dream, but when I saw the name that appeared on my caller ID, I smiled wide and rushed to answer. "Perfect timing. I was just having a very exciting dream about you and Willy."

Liam's deep chuckle reverberated over the line, and my heart practically melted at the sound. "Now *that* is an image I can go to bed with. Thanks, love."

A yawn followed his words, causing me to frown. "Have you slept at all?"

"Not a wink. It's been nonstop since I arrived. Sorry for not ringing earlier. I'm surprised production hasn't taken my phone by now."

"They can do that?"

"They can, and they will. My guess is Bart will take it before my interview today."

I chuckled. "Ahh, Bart. I bet he was a joy to see again."

Liam snorted. "I refer to him as my handler when we're together. Today was a strange day. As annoying as the bloke is,

I'm stuck with him until the end." I could hear the frustration in Liam's voice—like a weight was being added to his shoulders and he was desperate to breathe again.

"Well, I'm sorry to hear that, but maybe this week won't be as bad as you think."

Liam made a noise. "I wish I could be as optimistic as you."

I hated the thought of anything sabotaging Liam's chance to move on. "What could possibly happen? You're done with the show, right? I thought you just had to answer some questions for the media to wrap up your contractual obligations."

"That should be all, but—" He paused slightly, and I wondered if Liam was trying to find the politically correct way to tell me what he was feeling. "It's always safe to expect the unexpected with this show."

I was still confused about where his doubts were coming from. "Have you talked to Bart about it?" Then I cringed, remembering his unsure thoughts about the guy. "I know he's your producer, but what is his role in all of this anyway?"

"Bart's job is to know my weaknesses and manufacture situations that will test me. It's what makes great television. Great television creates buzz, and the more buzz, the better the ratings." He let out a heavy sigh. "Anyway, I don't want to burden you with the drama. If you don't hear from me until this circus is over, you know why. They'll take my phone. They'll shut it off, then they'll put me up in a bugged flat so they can track every move I make."

"You're kidding." I was legitimately appalled at what he was saying.

They really were treating him like a prisoner.

"I'm afraid not, love."

I couldn't ignore the heavy disappointment that fell over me. It wasn't enough that Liam was on an entirely different continent, but we couldn't even speak? "I wish I'd known all that."

"What would you have done, flown here with me?"

I knew he was teasing, but that was exactly what I was thinking. "Maybe I should have taken you seriously when you asked. It's just—"

"Everything was moving so fast?"

The fact that he finished my thought, especially considering the topic at hand—us—made me know that we were exactly on the same page. My heart swelled with feelings that I wasn't really expecting. Sure, Liam and I had spent a month getting to know each other and had only gotten closer in the last couple of weeks, but all this distance made me realize just how strong my feelings for him were.

"If it makes you feel any better," he said, interrupting my thoughts, "you'd be miserable here alone. I'd be busy the entire time then knackered at the end of each day. It's best you stayed home."

"Well then, when you put it like that…" I trailed off as my mind started to go wild. I hated that a part of me wondered if there was another reason for him to not want me there during the madness.

"Enough about all that," Liam said, changing the subject. "How was yesterday after I left?"

"Exhausting." I found my smile again as a visual of my last night with Liam played out in my mind. "I worked on some edits and watched the girls until bedtime. Then I crashed. Are you heading to bed now?"

Rustling filled the line. "Just dropped my pants."

A laugh slipped past my throat as I bit my bottom lip and rolled to my side to hug my pillow. I wished I were there to see that—to keep him awake, to help him fall asleep.

"I miss you." I kept my voice gentle despite the nerves

rattling around in my chest. "I know it's only been a day, but I wanted you to know."

The line crackled. At first, I thought I might have lost him, then his voice came through. "I miss you too."

When silence stretched between us again, more doubt crept through my mind. "Are you sure everything's okay over there?"

"It's just—I don't know what's going to happen this week. These interviews could get pretty intense and—I can't stomach the thought of you feeling less for me."

His words hit me straight in the gut. "I would never think less of you, Liam. But what are you asking of me?"

"Your understanding, I guess."

"Liam, I already understand you have a past and that there's a contract at stake here. It's only one week."

"One week of torture," he said.

"You can't think of it like that, and you need to stop being so hard on yourself. You're a good man, and you made the right decision for you. They'll see that in your interviews. They'll see exactly who you are in your truth. Your heart is your greatest weapon."

Silence sat between us, and I hated that Liam wasn't there with me, where I could look into his eyes and carry his pain with him. I didn't want him to be alone.

"All right, wise one." He spoke so softly, but I could hear the smile in his voice. It was contagious.

"Get some sleep, okay? Call tomorrow if they don't take your phone."

"Try to stop me," he teased. "Bye, love. Talk soon."

He hung up, and I felt wide awake. After an invigorating shower, I stepped into a light jogging outfit and headed to Spill the Tea. When I got there, it was still too early for the tearoom to be open, so I knocked on the glass and waved at my mom and dad when they looked up. My mom practically leapt to the door, causing me to laugh.

She let me in and locked the door behind me before facing me with a stern look. "You've been avoiding me."

I cringed with my smile and wrapped my arms around her. "I'm sorry. After word got out about Liam, I couldn't say much. I still can't believe Gwen posted what she did on social media. She had no business doing that."

"Oh, I agree. Although," my mom started with a light laugh, "business has been tremendous. Your dad and I have been swamped with to-go orders and a packed house every day since that post went viral. I'm not saying I'm happy about Liam's situation, but it's been a long time since we didn't have to watch the redline. It feels good."

A lump filled my throat when I tried to swallow again. My parents never talked finances with me, but I always had a feeling they were barely making ends meet. They never advertised. Their prices were always too cheap, and they could never afford to hire an employee to cover for them on the odd occasion that one of them couldn't work. It had always caused me an inkling of worry, so to hear my mom get so excited over business definitely played on my emotions.

I circled my palm on my mother's back. "You deserve all the attention. Just think, with all these new customers, that will mean more word of mouth and more new customers. You might need to finally break down and hire someone."

She giggled. "Oh dear." She playfully slapped my wrist. "It's only been a week. I'm sure it will die down once they realize Liam is back in London."

I didn't want my mom to think visitors were only coming into Spill the Tea to see if they could spot Liam. "You never know, Mom. Give yourself some credit. You do make the best scones and faux creme on this side of the pond." I smiled. "Word of mouth is everything."

She gave me a satisfied smile and tugged me to the counter. "Now that you're here, I want to hear the story. Everything."

I chose to be reserved in the information I gave her. Gwen was still her friend, and it wasn't like Liam was there with me now. We were in two different countries, living our lives, and hoping for something we could one day share. I didn't want to get my mom's hopes up, but I told her about some of our dates and the gentleman he was. I even threw in the story about how he scared off Dean, which had her giggling all over again.

"Well," my mom said after I told her about his request that I join him in London. "If it were me and your father in this same situation when we first started dating, I would have gone."

"You would have? Just like that? After only knowing him for a month?" I reeled back. "It all feels too fast to fly to another country for a guy."

My mom made a face. "Not if that guy is Liam Colborn."

"Wait a second." I laughed. "Two weeks ago you thought Liam was everything the media portrayed him to be. What did you call him? A coward and a prick?"

She visibly turned red then waved a hand in front of her face. "Nonsense. If I did say something of that sort, that was before I realized I knew him."

The way my mom feigned innocence had me biting back more laughter.

"But you don't know him."

She put her hands on her hips in a posture that told me she was ready to scold me. "He was a regular of mine and very sweet. The media has it all wrong, but they'll catch on. Just you wait."

I smiled, loving how fiercely my mother already loved Liam.

My phone rang, and I excused myself to grab it. My mom went to fuss behind the register, counting cash in the drawer and tidying up before it was time to open the tearoom.

My brows bent at the strange number on my caller ID until I realized it was a number from another country. "Oh my gosh. It's him." My heart was racing as I rushed to answer the call. He'd mentioned that his phone would get taken away. Maybe he'd found another way to get ahold of me. My cheeks were hurting from smiling so big.

"Hello."

"Yes, hello. Is this Chelsea Banks?"

Disappointment sank low in my gut. "This is she."

"Sorry to bother, miss. My name is Bart Landers. I'm Liam's producer from *British Bachelor*. I'm calling to talk to you about Liam, if that's all right."

My heart leapt into my throat. "Is he okay?"

A chuckle floated over the line. "Yes, miss. He's all right. However, he's told me quite a lot about you, and I gather that you might feel the same about him?"

And now every organ in my body was officially melting to the floor. "Of course I do."

It was in that next breath that I caught myself for talking to a complete stranger about my relationship with Liam. Who was this man? If he was the same Bart that Liam had been dealing with over the last week, then I probably shouldn't have trusted a word he said.

"I'm sorry." I laughed through my discomfort. "Why are you calling me instead of Liam?"

"Yes, to the point. Poor Liam has been through the

wringer lately, and the network would love to put a smile on his face. Would you be interested in taking a trip to London?"

The first thing I thought of was how I wanted nothing more than to be with Liam during this crazy time. But then I remembered what Liam had said about it being best that I wasn't there. "I mean, I would love to, but I don't think that's what Liam wants right now."

"Nonsense," Bart exclaimed. "Well, it's meant to be a surprise, but by the way he speaks about you, I know he'll be delighted to see you."

"Won't he be too busy?"

"Oh yes, he'll be terribly busy, but with you by his side, maybe it wouldn't be so bad. We'll pay for your ticket, put you up in a hotel, take care of your room service, and arrange transportation to wherever you'd like to go."

Bart's offer was generous. More than generous. Maybe Bart wasn't as bad of a guy as Liam thought. And after hearing Liam's frustration this morning, all I wanted to do was be with him. The offer was more than tempting. *Why should I sit back and wait for Liam?* I was going to go to him.

33

LIAM

The three days after my arrival became a monotony of recycled questions, vague answers, and a whole lot of wasted time—time I could have been spending with Chelsea and figuring out my next career move. In the rare moments of silence that fell on me between media appearances, I couldn't stop thinking about all the things I could do once I fulfilled my contract with the network, when the chains were finally broken and I was free to live a life away from the camera's eye.

Ever since my talk with Chelsea about the possibility of becoming a swim instructor and owning a tattoo shop, I'd felt excited about the future. It finally felt like a blank page ready to be written and filled with new dreams. Just a few more days of this madness, then it would be over for good.

I had to applaud myself. So far, I'd managed to stay on track giving everyone what they wanted—interviewers, fans of the show, and the network.

Bart proved to be useful in keeping my spirits up and

reminding me that the press tour would all be over soon. And so far, even I was pleased with how well it was going.

My anxiety dwindled quickly over having to dig a little deeper while speaking to the media about Blake and how his tragedy had changed me as a man and as someone who sought love. It actually started to become cathartic to talk about. Yes, I'd had a rough time after his death, especially once my Olympic career had faded into the background after my injury. The media embraced my story and started to spin me in a completely different light.

We were currently in the back of the company-provided car, on our way to a late-night talk show, *Good Evening with Hannah*. Bart was prepping me with questions, as he always did, when I noticed something felt different.

"Why aren't we sticking with our regular questions for this one?"

Bart looked up from his phone, where he was reading off the questions. "That happens after the same questions have been answered multiple times. It's all normal. Interviewers who are doing their homework won't want to put regurgitated questions out there, so they'll change it up a bit. Nothing to worry about."

Something still didn't sit right. I waved it away as the nerves that came with going off script. I'd just gotten comfortable with the press tour. I could see the light at the end of the tunnel. Now it felt like I was teetering off balance, and I didn't like it one bit.

"Just be on your toes, and try to stay close to the answers we've already discussed. You'll be fine."

I shifted my gaze to the roof of the car and sighed. His instructions to be vague were getting boring, but I knew it was better than elaborating and opening the door to more questions.

As I looked out the window, disappointment only added to my growing anxiety. I wished I could ring Chelsea. She always had a special knack for putting my mind at ease. I needed that now more than ever. Instead, I thought about what time it would be back in Providence and tried to guess what she was doing. She was probably busy with the twins or working on her book or taking a swim in that saggy one-piece ensemble I loved so much.

Whatever it was, I hoped she would stay off social media as much as possible. When I saw her again, I wanted us to start with a clean slate.

We arrived at the back door of the building thirty minutes before my interview time, and I was rushed straight to a dressing room, where I was told to wait until someone came to get me. Looking around at the plain brown couch and vanity mirror against one wall, I felt like the room was more like a holding cell than a dressing room. They didn't even have a television for me to watch the live filming.

Everything about the evening felt off, and I couldn't shake the vibe as I downed a bottle of water. After using the restroom and giving myself a once-over in the mirror, I jumped around a bit to try to shake my nerves. A quick tap on the door came twenty minutes later before it opened, and a man wearing a microphone on his head stepped into the room.

"Liam Colborn, you're on deck."

Bart clapped me on the back as I walked by him before he followed me out to the side stage, where we waited in the wings. A few minutes later, a video reel of my time on *British Bachelor* played, then the hosts were making my introduction to the audience. Just as the welcome applause started along with music from the live band, I was ushered out to the stage.

I put on my smile and waved to the crowd, the routine

beginning to feel so natural it was almost robotic. Considering I was functioning on five hours of sleep, I was most certainly operating like a robot.

The questions started out the same as any other interview. Thankfully, the hosts were as funny as they were serious, and there was a good mixture throughout the start, but that feeling in my gut continued to gnaw away with every minute that ticked on.

"I have to say," Hannah said, her body perfectly poised, her blond hair in a short bob around her head. "Your story is fascinating. Between the tragic loss of your brother, Blake, followed by your time in the Olympics that ended in a career-ending accident, you were so young and endured so much loss. I imagine that loss had to have tied into your time on the show."

"Learning about death at such a young age hardened me some," I admitted with a nod. "But instead of going down a darker path, avoidance was a coping mechanism that worked for me." As I spoke the words, my heart tightened in my chest. Talking and thinking about my brother had always been difficult, but to explore those feelings with the entire world was something entirely different.

"Is that what swimming was to you? A way to cope?"

I shrugged. "Absolutely. Don't get me wrong. I loved to swim. I still do, but it became an addiction that masked my grief. For years, I pushed my internal pain aside for that adrenaline rush. I pushed myself too hard and eventually —broke."

Hannah's sympathetic eyes were wide and glistening with unshed tears. "Wow, Liam. While I think it's natural for everyone who goes through pain like that to find ways to cope, I find it admirable that you've overcome so much. Then you got back out in the public's eye to find love. Why did you choose to do that?"

Memories of that time before the show came flooding back with her question. "Looking back, I knew there was something missing in my life. I was intrigued by the offer to find love in such a unique way. It just felt right, and I didn't hesitate to accept."

"So, it wasn't some publicity stunt, like some of the critics are saying? Liam Colborn was truly looking for love?"

I let out a light laugh. "I was definitely looking for love."

"Your end on the show was quite shocking to us all. You already mentioned how your brother's death taught you to cope in unhealthy ways. Do you feel you've learned anything from this experience? From being on the show and the aftermath of your decisions?"

I only had to think about that one for a second before launching into my answer. "Disappearing like that wasn't the best solution to the problem, and I fully acknowledge that I hurt many people in the process. I'm back here to help us all move forward. In a way, the show forced me to take a look at myself and what I wanted out of life, not just relationships. I don't think anyone can find a deep, meaningful love unless they're happy within themselves first. When I signed on to be the British Bachelor, I was lost and influenced by a life of avoidance."

"And now?" Hannah asked, the frown lines in her forehead coming together. "Do you think you've changed?"

I shifted, growing uncomfortable in my skin. "I wouldn't say I've changed as much as I've gained perspective."

An easy smile rested on Hannah's face. "I love that. So, where does that perspective bring you today, Liam? Will you continue to seek love out in the real world?"

Chelsea popped into my mind at that moment. If I was

seeking anything at all, it was a way back to her, to Providence, to my new future. "I'll never give up on love."

Hannah's mouth twisted into a smile, and the gleam of mischief in her eyes put me on high alert. "Considering the rumors circulating that you were with a woman in Providence, I assume you might have already found that love you've been searching for. Is there anything you can tell us about this mystery woman?"

Shit, shit, shit. My eyes shifted to the side stage, where Bart had been standing, but he was nowhere to be seen. I swallowed and turned back to Hannah. "No, I'm afraid not."

Hannah leaned forward, adopting a curious look. "So, you don't know a Chelsea Banks from Providence, Rhode Island?"

What the fuck? "I—um. Yes, I know Chelsea."

"And she's your…" Hannah prodded with an imploring smile.

Panic shot through me. "Friend." The word came out so fast, my only thought being that I didn't want to drag Chelsea into all the drama. To protect her. To keep her to myself. She didn't belong in this messed-up world I had lived in for so long.

"Just a friend?" Hannah pushed again, her expression telling me she didn't believe my lie one bit.

Anger bubbled inside me. I wasn't going to give Hannah or anyone else information. I'd meant it when I'd told Vince and everyone in that executive meeting that Chelsea Banks was off-limits.

"Chelsea is a good friend and nothing more."

"Nothing more? Are you sure?" This time, Hannah sat back, looking genuinely confused at my reaction, making me wonder what exactly she'd been told and by whom.

"Yes," I said, trying hard not to grit my teeth. "Nothing more."

Hannah could piss off before I told them a single thing about Chelsea, but my mind was racing. I didn't know how they'd gotten her name. None of the other interviewers had even mentioned her.

"Well," Hannah continued. It was like she was struggling with whatever information she had and hesitated to go on with the interview. She tapped at the microphone in her ear and shook her head. "I'm sorry, Liam. I must be mistaken. Let's move on, shall we?"

I nodded as a whoosh of relief passed through me until a second later, when I heard the audience collectively gasp. As I looked out at them to see what had caused their reaction, I saw fingers pointing and mouths dropping, their eyes on something behind me. I turned to find a large television screen behind her lighting up with a photo of Chelsea sitting between my legs at the park while I kissed her cheek. It was the same photo from the meeting three days ago.

Everyone in the audience was talking loudly, and boos were being tossed out from the crowd. I'd been set up. By the look on Hannah's face, she'd been set up too.

It was the only explanation for the confusion, but why? This was not part of the deal. My gaze turned back to the side stage, where Bart stood again, but this time he wasn't alone. As soon as I saw Chelsea standing there with him, her face appearing stricken and her eyes bloodshot with pain, I knew without a doubt it was Bart who had arranged everything.

"This interview is over," I choked out. Then I stood and ripped the microphone from my body before throwing it back on the couch. I hurried toward Chelsea, who took off down the hall.

"Well," Hannah said with an awkward laugh behind me. "That sure went a different direction than I was expecting."

As soon as I passed Bart, whose expression was unreadable, I pointed a finger at him and glared. "You wanker."

Looking down the hall to where a flash of red caught my eye, I saw her gaining traction toward the exit. My heart instantly plummeted into my stomach. She couldn't leave before I had a chance to explain.

"Chelsea."

Her red locks bobbed around her shoulders as she ran, my heart breaking with every step she took. She was almost to the exit.

"Chelsea!"

34

Who flies to London for a man they've only known for a month? My red heels click-clacked against the concrete floor as I raced down the hall of the studio building. I'd been a fool a million times over for rearranging everything in my life, all to visit a man who thought of me as just a friend. *Nothing more.*

He sure hadn't acted like I was *nothing* to him all those nights he'd spent in my bed. But it wasn't the sex that bothered me. It was the fact that I'd come to London because I'd been falling in love with a man who I'd thought might feel the same way about me.

"Chelsea!"

I heard Liam calling my name. I heard his heavy steps as they chased me down the mazelike hall, but I didn't look over my shoulder toward the voice until my hand was on the door. There he was, running toward me, his expression undeniably apologetic for what I'd heard him say. With an annoyed breath, I turned to face him.

Liam's breathing was heavy, his skin flushed from the workout, and his eyes too wide for his face. "What are you—" he started, but he caught himself with a squeeze of his lids.

"What am I doing here? I came to surprise you, Liam. But I guess that's not something a *friend* would normally do, huh?"

He shook his head as if his own word pained him. "You're much more than a friend. You know that."

I narrowed my eyes, my heart shredding at my doubt. "Do I? You really expect me to trust you after what you said out there. How can I?"

"Don't you understand? I never wanted you involved in this show. This is what these people do. They catch me off guard and parade my weaknesses around like I'm a toy. You're my weakness, and they knew it."

My chin shook with all the emotion racking my body. Everything he said was the right thing and exactly what I wanted to hear, but I couldn't stop the pain that came with overhearing him tell the world that I was nothing more than his friend. "I don't know how to believe you right now."

He let out a sigh, his chest deflating with defeat. "You promised me you could never think less of me."

My throat felt swollen as my entire body shook. "Yeah, well maybe that was before I realized that *you* think less of *me*." I let out a half groan, half scream. "You know what's funny? I could have actually been your friend back in Providence if that was what you wanted, but you just kept pushing for more, didn't you?" A tear slipped down my cheek, and I sucked in a shaky breath. "You should have left me alone."

He reached for my arm and tugged me closer. "Don't do this. Don't make me the villain in your life too."

I shook my head, my eyes wet and tired. "I didn't do that. You did that to yourself. To us. And now it's over."

I pulled back to find an entire crew packed in the hallway

with Bart, Hannah, and two giant black cameras. Liam turned in the direction my eyes were pointed, and his expression went from pained to furious in less than a second.

"What the bloody hell is this?" Liam's boom reverberated down the halls and probably out to the stage and audience. "Get out of here."

He shoved the lens of a camera away from his face while I just stood there—shocked, mortified, heartbroken, confused. And lucky for me, it had all just been caught on camera.

"You don't have my permission to record me." My anger was directed at Bart, my voice shaky but firm.

Bart waved his hands in front of the camera, instructing them to shut down, but it was Hannah who stepped forward to take everyone to a commercial break.

Bart turned back to us and folded his arms across his chest with a sigh. "You signed permission before entering the studio, love, but this wasn't at all how I thought it would go down."

Liam gawked at him. "What did you expect bringing her into this after I specifically told you not to?"

Bart shook his head. "I don't know, Liam. I thought you would be happy, excited, surprised." He raked a frustrated hand through his hair. "Bollocks."

Liam was yelling at Bart, so I took the opportunity to slip out the exit, hoping to make a clean break, but Liam was right on my tail.

"Chelsea, stop. Don't leave like this."

I sucked in a deep breath as his arms wrapped around me and pulled me in. When I inhaled his familiar scent, I sighed almost immediately. He felt the same as he had before he left for London. His scent was the same too. And just like that, I could feel the calm that came with being with Liam. The eye of the storm before it swept us up into its wrath. I wanted to hold onto that moment, to go back to everything before this night.

"You need to do what you came here to do, Liam." I looked up into his eyes. Though mine were still blurry, his pleading expression remained. "You were right to tell me to stay away from this world. I want no part of the lies. This isn't reality." I shook my head and let out a laugh. "Then again, who am I to tell you what's real and what's fiction when I don't even know myself anymore."

A car pulled up behind me, and after quickly verifying it was mine, I pushed Liam's hands off of me and turned to get in. This time, he didn't come after me, and I felt like we were separated by more than just a continent.

Everything leading up to my arrival at the studio had felt like it was moving in triple speed. After walking away from Liam, everything immediately slowed down.

I was in a daze, drifting from the car to the flat provided by Bart when he'd set this whole scandal up. I was certain of one thing. I wouldn't make any decisions that night. I would sleep off my jet lag, order an insane amount of room service whenever I awoke, then I would figure out my next move.

Deep inside my heart, I knew I couldn't let these next few days pass in vain. *Easy* was the route I'd taken too often in my life, from dating the wrong men far longer than I should to neglecting to tell my parents my decisions about school because I didn't want to hear their disappointment or by rewriting a book six times instead of publishing the damn thing. Something had to change. It might as well start here and now.

By the time I finally woke, nearly twelve hours had passed.

Two in the afternoon with a fresh mind and clear eyes looked and felt a whole lot different than at two in the morning after getting my heart broken in front of a live audience. I could easily spend my afternoon dwelling on the previous night, but instead, I made the decision to go a different route.

My lips flattened as irritation ran through me, and I picked up the phone.

"Room service," announced the woman on the other end of the line.

"Hi, I'd like to place an order." I ran my eyes down the list of food from the room service menu and stopped at an item priced at one hundred and eighty pounds. "Your caviar omelet looks delightful. Do you recommend it?"

The woman on the other end of the line choked on her words for no other reason, I guessed, than the price. "Absolutely, ma'am. The omelet is our highest-rated item from our five-star kitchen. You'll be delighted with your choice."

"Wonderful." My smile grew wider. "I would love to try it and…" I looked to the next page where the drinks were mentioned. "A bottle of your most expensive champagne as well."

"Yes, ma'am. Would you like some juice with your champagne?"

I perked up at the thought of having a mimosa. "Yes, please. Orange juice would be fantastic."

"All right, miss. You're all set. We'll be up as soon as it's ready."

My order arrived less than fifteen minutes later, courtesy of *British Bachelor*, and I was happy to find that the food was more than worth the price, especially considering I wasn't the one who would foot the bill.

After one glass of champagne, I placed the bottle back in the bucket of ice and decided to save the rest for the evening.

Then I showered, changed, and headed out on the town without a plan—and with a map to help me navigate my way.

I knew little about London, other than what I'd learned from my driver and the bit of information Liam had told me. I knew that the cute townhome-styled hotel I was staying at was in the district of Kensington in central London. From there, my options seemed endless.

According to the colored lines on my map, I could hop on the tube at the nearest underground station and head west into Notting Hill or east toward Tower Hill, where I could walk the River Thames and catch sight of the London Bridge, Big Ben, and the Tower of London. All the things Brendan had been so excited to see on his trip there with the family.

I didn't know if I would ever have this opportunity again, so I went on a hunt for the tube, purchased an Oyster card, and made my way east on the District line.

My nerves rattled with every step I took. Walking around a foreign city alone was more terrifying than I'd prepared for. What if I ended up traveling in the wrong direction and got lost? I only had two hundred pounds on me, which upon my arrival, I'd thought would be plenty. But in uncharted territory, my pulse wouldn't stop racing at all the what-ifs.

I was grateful for the fear that pumped through my veins as I exited the tube and headed up the escalator toward the river. Anything to distract me from recent events. But as soon as I reached the sidewalk at the top of the steps, I froze, causing the people on my heels to mutter curse words and walk around me.

My eyes landed on a huge billboard on the side of a red bus with Liam's smiling face holding a bundle of red roses in the shape of a heart.

Suddenly, everything I'd felt last night slammed into me. My sadness mixed with the anxiety of being so far from home became an overwhelming rush of emotion that I had no idea what to do with. Tears flooded my eyes as I held onto the stair rail for support. I had tried to be so strong, but now, all I could think about was how, even though I *could* be alone, it hadn't been what I wanted at all. I'd wanted to experience all of this for the first time with Liam.

At my realization, I continued onto the sidewalk and slipped into the nearest pub. Its dark wood and Victorian architecture screamed comfort in my moment of darkness. I sat on a stool at the bar and stared at the television until the bartender finally made his way over to me.

After ordering a glass of wine, my gaze returned to the television. The local news was playing, and I found that the drama in the world, which was far more important than my own heartbreak, helped to push thoughts of Liam away.

Every now and then, I would get slightly paranoid and swear that someone was staring at me from somewhere in the bar. But then when I would look at them, they would turn their head so fast that it made me wonder if I'd just had too much to drink.

It was silly to think my face would be recognizable from the photos that had leaked after they'd aired last night or from the video that had exposed just how much Liam's words had hurt to hear. Then again, it was silly for me to fly all the way to London only to find myself in a pub, alone, in the middle of the foreign city.

"Another pinot?" the bartender asked, reaching for my empty glass.

"Oh yes," I said with a nod. "And pizza. Do you have pizza?"

The man smiled and shook his head. "Afraid not, love. You've come to the wrong pub if you want pizza." He slid a menu to me, and I frowned at the millionth reminder of how far away from home I was.

"Okay then, what do you recommend?"

As he started to rattle off popular menu items, a voice on the television screen caught my attention, and I looked up. It was a commercial for the reunion episode of *British Bachelor* that would be airing live tonight.

My chest tightened as I focused back on the bartender. I shook my head and pushed the menu back toward him. "I think I'll stick with wine."

Life had an interesting way of flipping me on my ass from time to time. I just hoped I wouldn't fall on mine by the time I ended up leaving this pub.

35

LIAM

I was living a nightmare, in a prison of my own making. What I'd become was worse than a robot. I was a man living the tale of my own lie, and I hated myself for it. Most of all, I hated what I'd done to Chelsea in the process.

It was the night of my final contractual obligation, the reunion show that had been all the buzz since my return last week. Everything I'd done over the last five days had prepped the viewers for what was to—in their eyes—be the showdown of the century. It would be drama in its finest form as the women I'd dumped on television came to confront me with their feelings.

I was ready for the punches that, at one point, even I'd thought I deserved. The audience and the women certainly thought that I did. But I'd accepted the fact that even though I'd only tried to follow the truth in my heart, I hadn't signed up for that. I'd signed up to very publicly date women with the expectation that I would pick the one I would want to spend forever with. Unfortunately, that woman hadn't been chosen for the show.

Bart stepped into my dressing room without knocking. "Good in here, mate?"

I gritted my teeth, ready to remind him that I wasn't his "mate," but he didn't give me time to speak. He knew I was still furious at him for the arrangements he'd made behind my back.

"I came to say the show is starting in thirty minutes. Colin will introduce the ladies, bring them out, have a quick chat, then we'll be calling to bring you out."

I nodded, refusing to speak to the man I'd once considered a friend.

He sighed, already fed up with the silent treatment I'd been giving him. "Right, well, this will all be over soon."

After what had happened the night before, my excitement for the show ending had faded. There was nothing to look forward to without Chelsea waiting for me on the other side of the camera. She was gone, and I had no idea where to start looking. Without my phone, I couldn't even attempt to track her down.

"This will all be over soon for you." I narrowed my eyes at Bart as I spoke. "But thanks to you, I'll be living this night-mare until Chelsea forgives me. You had no right to contact her behind my back."

Bart shook his head. "It's my job, Liam, and I'm damn good at it. You might not like my methods, but if you hadn't said what you said last night, you and Chelsea would probably be shagging right here, right now. *You* mucked that up, not me. Take some accountability for once."

Without another word, he slipped out the door and slammed it behind him.

Talk about sitting in the hot seat. Every eye in the room was focused on me for the majority of the segment. The cast of women sat on a bleacher-style setup off the edge of the main stage while the host of *British Bachelor*, Colin, sat across from me on an oversized chair.

Thanks to my month-long holiday after the show, everyone seemed to be wound up for the grand showdown. The pent-up anger was apparent from the moment I stepped on stage, and the crowd started to boo, clap, cheer—the greeting was a healthy mixture of all the above.

The women were as heated and as pissed as ever. Colin was definitely playing up the sympathy card. The audience's oohs and aahs were perfectly timed. And I just sat there, feeling like a complete arse, listening as they vocalized their frustrations with me as they recapped dates they thought had gone perfectly.

Video reminders of every single breakup played throughout the show, only digging a deeper hole in the wounds I'd created. I'd never apologized so much in my entire life, and while I couldn't be sure how genuine the women were, I was genuine in my apologies. It had never been my intention to hurt anyone.

We'd just gotten back from a commercial break when Colin invited Francesca onto the stage to join us. The crowd clearly loved her. She'd received the loudest applause when first introduced at the start of the show, and the crowd rose to their feet when she headed over to the couch.

I stood and hugged her, the same as I'd done with all the other women that had joined me. "Nice to see you again," I muttered. In a way, it was good to see her again. After all, she'd played a huge part of my time on the show, time when I'd genuinely started to have feelings for her.

"Sure it is," was her response. So dry, so cold. I was

surprised to see the warm smile on her face when we pulled apart.

She turned and blew kisses to the audience, followed by a princess wave, then we both sat down. I hadn't expected to feel my blood boil at any of my interactions with the women, but when I saw Francesca playing the audience just like she'd played me on camera during production, I was reminded of how our off-camera time had gone on our last night together.

"Is this the first time you two have spoken or seen each other since the show?" Colin asked, faux curiosity written all over his face. He already knew the answer to that.

Francesca and I both agreed that it was, in fact, our first time speaking, but then Francesca decided to take it even further. "It's just so strange to see someone every day and to be so sure you're going to marry that person, and then they just disappear off the face of the earth."

Francesca pouted just slightly to get a sympathetic reaction from the crowd.

"What do you have to say to that, Liam?" Colin asked, keeping the perfect balance of imploring and sensitive.

"Well," I started while I turned to face Francesca. "I suppose everything became strange after-the-fact. Breaking things off was hard for me too."

She pushed her lips out farther in a bigger pout. "But *you* broke up with *me*."

"That doesn't mean I enjoyed it, Francesca. People break up every day. You date, you get to know people, then you either stay together or you break up."

I cringed, realizing that could come off sounding heartless in the situation. I'd been reminded every day for the past three months that I'd broken women's hearts. When could I finally move on?

"But that's what I don't understand," she said, shifting on

the couch to face me straight on. "Our dates were amazing. We got along so well."

"On the surface, yes."

Everyone in the room sucked in a breath while Francesca's mouth hung open, like she'd just been slapped.

"Look," I said, turning to Colin. "Every single woman sitting here tonight deserves to find love. The perfect, magical, amazing kind of love that comes along once in a lifetime. I couldn't give that, even when I thought I could. Throughout this entire process, I learned more about myself than I ever had in my life. Making that lifelong commitment is a big deal, and I would have done every woman here a disservice if I had picked them." I turned my glance to the group of women sitting offstage. "Sometimes, it's just not meant to be. That wasn't something I could control or predict, and I'm very sorry I couldn't be that person."

I was more than surprised when a round of applause came from the audience. My eyes searched the crowd to see nodding heads, like I'd finally said something they understood. I was finally being honest.

"It doesn't matter what you say now," Francesca said with an incredulous look on her face. "You've had a month to prepare for this reunion. Emotions aren't nearly as high as they were when the show ended."

I took a deep breath, trying to control my rising annoyance. All I wanted was to walk off the stage, take my phone back from production, and find Chelsea, whether she was back in America or still in London. I had to find her, and the longer this interview carried on, the harder that would be.

"I'm very sorry, Francesca."

"Clearly, you're not," she pushed. "You said you've learned so much from being on the show and that you've gained perspective, yet even when you're off the show, you're breaking women's hearts."

I tilted my head, trying desperately to hold onto my wits at her subtle mention of Chelsea. "It's a little impossible to break someone's heart when that heart was never yours to begin with. You never loved me, Francesca."

Francesca's jaw dropped. "And what do *you* know about love? You had thirty chances here, and then you broke up with us all, ran to Providence, and snuck around with some— nanny?" Her voice was practically squealing when she was done.

I pressed down on my ear with my pointer finger and wiggled it a bit, hoping to stop the ringing. By the time I regained my hearing, I felt like I was ready to explode. "Yes, as a matter of fact, that's exactly what happened, and you know what I realized?" I looked to Colin. "I'm not the bad guy. You can all paint me as the villain if that's what you need to do, but I joined this show for the right reasons. Because I wanted to find love. And you know what? It actually worked. I found love. Not in the way you all expected or wanted, but I found her, and I'll do anything to get her back."

"Wait a second," Colin said, looking as confused as ever. "Are you saying that you're in love with *the nanny*?"

My lids fell shut as annoyance raged through me. Then I thought of Chelsea's face. Her presence that had always steadied me when I least expected it. I opened my eyes and smiled. "First of all, her name is Chelsea. And not only am I in love, but I finally understand the meaning behind that phrase."

The audience gasped and talked amongst themselves, even while the stage crew tried to silence them with frantic waves of their hands.

"I thought she was just your friend," Colin said, still trying to understand.

"She is my friend, my best friend, but I never should have reduced her to just that. She's my soul mate, my everything, and I need to find her."

I stood up from the couch and looked down at Colin, my hand moving to the microphone inside the back of my trousers. I was so desperate to remove the microphone that I barely noticed Colin announcing the commercial break.

"Can we help?"

Colin's question more than surprised me. "Really?"

He nodded and stood up, clapping his hand on my shoulder. "Well, yeah, bud. If there's a love story here, I think we all want in on it." He turned to the audience, even though the cameras were off, since they could still hear. "Right guys?"

The audience roared with their applause.

As exciting as the enthusiasm was, I still had a major dilemma. "Well, alright. But I have no idea where to start looking. She could have gone back to America for all I know."

"She hasn't checkout out of the hotel, mate. She's still in London."

We all swiveled toward Bart's voice coming from side stage.

I ground my teeth and nodded, finally accepting Bart's part in all of this. He was here for the ratings, and if that meant helping me get the girl in the end, then he would do it.

"Alright," I said. "But I'll need my mobile back first."

Bart slipped his hand in his pocket, pulled out my phone, and tossed it to me. "Thought you might ask for that." Then he winked. "Fully charged."

Colin chuckled then snapped his fingers to someone on the side of the stage. "I think we can help you out with that." He stood and held out his hand to shake mine. "Let's go find Chelsea, shall we? I can't wait to meet your girl."

36

CHELSEA

A t some point between late afternoon and after dark, the pub I'd chosen to wallow in became busy with customers. Mostly, they'd taken up the seating in the dining room, but the bar area was packed now too. I sat, stubbornly drowning myself in wine that just kept coming. I even made friends with the group of girls that crowded behind my stool as we all watched the train wreck that was the *British Bachelor Reunion*.

It turned out, every female in freaking London knew the show, and Liam, well. And when they asked me if I was "that Chelsea girl," it didn't even phase me to lie and tell them no, especially not with four glasses of wine in me.

"That wanker, Francesca, wants to be the British Bachelorette," commented one of my new friends. "She's eating this up. Just look at her."

I tried to focus on the screen, and on the flawless Francesca, but I was too hyped up to focus on one thing at that given moment. Exhaustion, the booze, and the lack of food in my body was a perfect storm for the painful hangover that awaited me in the morning. I didn't care. If it dulled the ache in my heart, then I was all for it.

"I thought she was just your friend," the host, Colin, said.

"She is my friend," Liam responded. "My best friend, but I never should have reduced her to just that. She's my soul mate, my everything, and I need to find her."

Near the end of Liam's speech, I started to think that maybe I was imagining his words. I'd imagined a lot of things over the past couple of days, and Liam proclaiming his love for me on television had definitely slipped into my fantasies. But just as quickly as I thought I heard him say the words, my denial swallowed me whole.

"Did you hear him? He loves you, Chelsea!" cried out another one of my new friends.

My laughter that followed came straight from my gut. "No," I said, whipping my head left then right. "I'm his *friend*. Nothing more." I believed what I was saying. I believed it with so much conviction that my heart broke all over again. Rolling my eyes, I took another sip of my wine then set it down before spinning on my stool and throwing up my arms. "Who wants a shot?"

My new friends cheered, and I ordered us a round of lemon drops. Eventually, I left my stool to play a round of pool with the girls. For a few minutes in time, I actually considered them real-life friends. It felt good to not feel so alone in London.

"Where is she?"

I was bent over the pool table, preparing to take my shot, when the familiar voice boomed from the entrance of the pub. My pulse took off racing. My heart crashed through my rib cage, and every muscle in my body froze while my gaze panned over to the door.

Every emotion I'd felt over the last few days rolled through me, a roller coaster of highs and lows and twists and turns, flipping and spiraling, until I didn't know which way was up. Liam was standing in the threshold of the pub, his eyes actively scanning every inch of the joint until they landed on me, and he immediately stepped forward.

I swallowed, my stomach somersaulting as my heart grew heavier in my chest. I was back on that damn roller coaster, on the upward climb of the world's tallest ride. The closer he got, the higher I went, every inch bringing me closer to the peak that would take me over the edge.

He stopped when he reached the pool table. Only worn green felt separated us. The girls I had been playing with were inching their way behind me, whispering words of encouragement. I didn't even care that cameras were following behind him.

"Hi."

At least that was what I thought he said by the way his lips moved. The pub was too loud to hear much. His expression carried so much remorse that my heart squeezed in my chest. He was still dressed in the same suit I'd seen him wearing on television less than an hour ago.

"Were you watching?" Liam shouted, his eyes flickering with hope.

It took me a second to sort through my alcohol-induced fog to realize he was talking about the reunion show.

And that was the when words he'd said—words I'd thought I'd imagined—came back to me full force. *She's my soulmate, my everything. And I need to find her.*

Had he really spoken those words on television for everyone to hear? I'd gone immediately into denial after he'd said them. I hadn't given it a second thought until now.

I still held the pool cue as I pulled myself up straight, realizing I hadn't responded to him. "You might need to repeat what you said!" I yelled. "I've had a lot of wine."

He let out a slight laugh before resting his hands on the edge of the pool table and leaning in. "I said you're my everything, my soul mate, and I love you. You have every right to be upset with me, but I won't allow this distance anymore."

My heart felt like it was in my throat while he spoke, every word he shouted penetrating deep in my soul and reverberating outward. I sucked in a breath and tilted my head, biting back on my smile as my throat thickened with emotion. "What? I'm sorry, I don't think I heard you."

He narrowed his lids, his gaze locked on mine as he started to move. My feet were still rooted as he made his way around the pool table, his right hand dragging along the edge until he was right in front of me. He towered above me, his chest flush to the top of my head, then he brought his hands up to cup my face while he lowered his to leave only a couple of inches between us.

"Can you hear me now?" This time, he didn't bother to shout. His words were gentle, sincere, and filled with a plea I couldn't ignore.

I nodded, my eyes already brimming with unshed tears. "Yes."

"Good. Because I love you, Chelsea Banks. And I really need you to forgive me for being a wanker last night. I was only trying to guard the one good thing in my life, but I realize now that you don't need protecting. You're capable of doing that all on your own. I promise to keep that in mind from now on. Just don't walk away from this." He placed his forehead on mine, closed his eyes, and exhaled in a steady stream.

I wrapped my arms around his waist, emotion bubbling up in my chest as I held back my tears. Placing my lips against his, I whispered shakily, "I love you too."

That was all the momentum we needed to tip over the edge of the track and begin the ride of our life. Together.

His lips slammed to mine, and the room erupted in a cheer so loud it made me smile. Liam demanded my full attention with a growl, kissing me harder as he hugged me tighter. My head spun. Wild butterflies became uncaged in my chest as I melted into him.

At some point during our kiss, Liam lifted me and wrapped my legs around his waist before pulling back slightly and smiling. "I guess this means I'm not the Forever Bachelor anymore. Think you can handle that responsibility?"

"What exactly does the job entail?"

He twisted his lips. "I'm afraid I left the job description at my flat. If you'd like to join me, I'd be more than happy to go over the details in private."

With a soft laugh, I darted a glance at the cameras that were only a few feet away now. Smiling, I turned back to Liam and bit down on my lip. "Considering this will probably be an *intense* negotiation, that would probably be best."

He set me down and clutched my hand, keeping me close as he pulled me toward the exit. Off we went, past the cameras, past the crowd, and not stopping until we reached his flat in Kensington, not too far from my hotel.

It was dark when we entered his apartment, and he didn't bother turning on a light before tugging me down the narrow hallway and through the double doors that led to his bedroom. We'd made out for the entire ride here, and my mind was still spinning from the high of it all. But from what I could see, his flat had a pristine nature that seemed to suit him well—with white walls, black accents, and natural wood grain surfaces. It was intriguing to see the way he lived since I'd only seen him outside of his natural habitat.

"What are you looking at?" Liam asked while unbuttoning his shirt.

"I realized that I've never seen you in your element. This place suits you." I replaced his busy fingers with my own, more than happy to undress the man who'd just professed his love to me in front of the entire world.

"That's nice, love, but I won't be here long."

I smiled, my heart quickening in my chest. "Got plans to move somewhere?"

His fingers slipped up my tank top to my bra and brushed over my nipple. "I hear Providence is nice, and the women are bloody fantastic."

"I can't argue with that," I said, slipping his shirt off him and tossing it to the side. I reached for his pants next. "Why don't you tell me more about this job offer?"

He lifted my tank top over my head and tossed it into a pile with his shirt. "Well," he said, slamming my hips to his, where I could feel him. "It's definitely going to be *hard* work."

I slipped my hand between us and wrapped my fingers around his dick. Sadly, it was still covered. That didn't stop me from feeling how hard he was. "So, you're looking for the right fit?"

His lips curled into a smile as his fingers dipped into the waistband of my skirt and started to pull it down. My skirt fell, and I kicked it away.

"Definitely," he said. "However, I'm willing to work with you for as long as it takes to ensure a smooth transition."

A laugh slipped past my throat, unable to help myself. He was so British, and so damn adorable, I couldn't take it anymore. "You sound like you're very hands-on with your employees. That's impressive." I squeezed his length one more time for good measure before pushing his pants and under-wear down to the floor, leaving him bare before me.

Liam released my bra next, his smile widening. "I do enjoy getting the job done, Miss Banks." He stepped forward and pushed me onto the bed, then pressed a knee on the mattress between my thighs. "Giving back to my employees is something I like to think I do very well." Then he leaned over my breast and took a swipe of my nipple with his tongue. "Especially when they taste like you." He proceeded to trail kisses down my breast, over my rib cage, and down my waist—but when he got to the line of my underwear, he froze. "Bloody fucking hell, you didn't."

I bit down on my lip to keep from bursting with laughter, loving his reaction to my new tattoo. "I did."

He was careful to pull my panties down over my hips, then he was examining me like I was newfound treasure. "It looks amazing. When did you do this?"

"The day before I decided to come here. It's still healing."

"It's perfect," he said, still staring at it, his mouth slack. Then he looked up, his eyes glistening in the soft light that came from the streetlamp outside his window. "*You're* perfect."

He crawled up my body and pressed his lips to mine. "I love you. And I'm not just saying that because I thought I was going to lose you. I started falling for you almost immediately. It was the scariest feeling in my life. For the first time, I feel like someone sees me for everything I aim to be in this life. You believe in me."

With all the crying I'd done over the past few days, I would have thought that I was all out of tears. Liam's words were the sweetest and most genuine words I could ever have hoped to hear. "Of course I believe in you, and you believe in me. Everything you said is exactly why I love you too. I'll always be your biggest fan."

His nose touched mine before he kissed me again and sighed. "And I'll always be yours."

He nudged my entrance, warning me only a second before pushing inside me, slowly, just like he'd promised. I focused on my breathing as he worked his way deeper, and I embraced the way my body spread just for him, like it had prepared for his arrival.

He'd gone as deep as he could go, and his thrusts started immediately after. "God, you feel so good," he growled, and his mouth fell to my neck. "I missed this. The way we fit is so bloody perfect."

His pace quickened with every rock of his body, and I knew that this fuck wouldn't be as gentle as our previous encounters. He'd missed me, and he was about to show me how much.

He flipped me on my side and entered me from behind with one hand finding my clit. He worked me from both angles, circling his finger over my sensitive bud while ramming me with his cock. It was a matter of seconds before I reached climax.

I cried out in warning, and he responded by grabbing my chin and twisting my head until his lips could reach mine. "Come for me, Chelsea. I need to feel you."

We only kissed a second before my orgasm hit me hard. I cried into his mouth, causing him to fuck me harder, not stopping until his juices were pumping inside of me, filling me to the brink.

When he flipped me onto my back, I was breathing heavily at the intensity of what had just gone down. Liam had never fucked me like that before, and I liked it a little too much. "Your job offer was phenomenal," I said while we chuckled.

"I do hope you'll accept the long-term position." He moved to hover over me, his mouth just an inch from mine.

Then he brushed a thumb against my cheek and smiled. "I promise to make it worth your while."

I smiled, ready to end the negotiations. "I accept."

EPILOGUE

Moving day, a day I had always viewed with contempt until today. I had been renting a flat in Providence for the past year, and before that I'd hopped around from flat to flat for years without ever feeling settled. After closing on my first house only a block away from the Hogues', I finally felt like I'd found home.

Admittedly, the location choice was a strategic move on my part to get Chelsea to move in with me. She only agreed on the condition that Simon and Bridget would keep her employed if she lived off-property. As much as they would have loved for Chelsea to stay close, they agreed that they would rather deal with the short distance if they could keep her. So, Chelsea and I were officially going to be roommates.

Between the two of us, we didn't have many possessions. One trip in the moving truck carried her bed, couch, television, clothes, record player, and several miscellaneous boxes of household items—most of them books that she had never been able to display with such a small shelf. Whatever we didn't have, we would shop for.

While Chelsea watched the twins all day, I took care of the move with Simon's help. I could afford the day off from the tattoo shop. I'd started leasing the suite in Wayland Square a few months ago, and the renovations were nearly done. I'd taken an assistant coaching position at one of the local high schools too. It wasn't what I'd been planning or expecting, but when the position became available, and I saw that it was part-time, and seasonal only, I went for it without hesitation.

Life was good, better than good, and today signaled yet another milestone in my life with Chelsea. Starting with my plan to have as much as possible in its place by the time Chelsea arrived. I had one more surprise for her.

After a quick shower, I threw on clean sweatpants and started to make dinner. One thing that had surprised Chelsea over the past year had been my skills in the kitchen. My Italian dishes were her favorite by far. I could tell because she always made moaning sounds that reminded me of her orgasms when she ate them. And then I'd eat her.

She was scheduled to arrive home the same moment I popped dinner in the oven and set the timer. For a final touch, I set out two glasses of her favorite red wine, lit a few candles, and started The 1975's album on her record player.

Almost as soon as I finished setting up, I heard the jostle of the doorknob and jogged to greet her, swinging the door open in a grand flourish.

"Welcome home, love."

She was all smiles, that pretty pink flush filling her cheeks and her thick hair tossed up in a crazy bun from playing with toddlers all day. "Oh my God, it smells amazing in here. You moved *and* you cooked?"

She walked right into my welcoming arms, her eyes busily scanning the space around me.

"That's right," I said. "You can help me fill in the blanks, but I think I did a pretty good job—with Simon's help, of course."

"We're definitely going to need to work on filling the blanks." She laughed and looked back at me with a tilt of her head. "I'm happy to help with that."

The home I'd ended up buying was definitely bigger than what Chelsea and I needed, but I'd fallen in love with the idea of everything it could be and more. Four bedrooms, three baths, a loft, a large kitchen with a spacious living room, and an office for Chelsea to write in. One day, we would fill it all.

She pulled me in for a kiss with so much passion behind it that I could feel it in my chest. Every day with Chelsea only made me more grateful for our awkward beginning. Before her, I didn't believe in soul mates or "the one," but every single day proved just how naive I'd been about love. Chelsea and I were the real deal. Forever. And I couldn't wait to spend the rest of my life with her.

When we pulled apart, I squeezed her waist. "Ready to see the house? Don't worry. I left the decorating up to you." I winked.

Chelsea jumped excitedly. "Yes. I can't wait."

I took her through the living room and kitchen, then showed her the den where I imagined her spending her days. She still hadn't decided what she wanted to do with the space, but I often caught her looking for inspiration online.

The tour was quick, considering there wasn't much to see, but I figured the last room I showed her would take the most time anyway. When we reached the door to the largest guest room, I stopped and stood in front of it, my heart racing. "You can consider what's in this room a welcome home present." I smiled, barely able to contain my excitement. I'd been planning this for months, and without Simon's help, there was no way I could have had it ready today.

Her eyes were wide, clearly already surprised. "What? You didn't tell me you were getting me a present."

I bit down on my lip before pushing open the door behind me. "I hope you like it."

She looked past me into the room, and I would never forget her reaction. It was better than the feeling of purchasing our new home. Her eyes flew open. Her hands rushed to her face, and she gasped so loud, my throat instantly clogged with emotion. It seemed she liked it.

She stepped into the room, scanning one wall at a time like she still couldn't believe what she was seeing. Wall-to-wall white bookshelves lined the room, and the books I'd unpacked from her boxes took up one complete wall. She turned to the next wall, which was empty, and she shook her head as a tear fell onto her cheek.

"Liam, this is—"

"Too much? Perfect? What, love?"

"It's all the things. It's a dream. There's even a ladder," she said with a shocked cry. "Oh my gosh, Liam, this is too much. And here I bought you a cactus."

I came up behind her, chuckling, and wrapped my arms around her waist. I pressed my mouth to her ear. "One day you can fill the shelves with all of your books."

She looked at me over her shoulder and held my face while she kissed me. "I couldn't love you more than I already do, but this is an incredible gift. Thank you."

I kissed her cheek and moved back to her ear, my heart hammering away at the last of my surprise. "There's one more thing." I turned her to face the final wall.

"What is—" She paused midquestion as she took in exactly what she was seeing.

Hundreds of copies of her second published book sat on the shelves with their spines facing out. I'd arranged them in the shape of a phrase that I imagined she'd finally made sense of when her body started to shake.

WILL
YOU
MARRY
ME?

She turned to find me kneeling before her, extending my hand that held a small black velvet box.

"Chelsea," I started, hoping to God that I could make it through my speech without completely losing it. "Every moment with you has been one I will cherish forever. From that first glance in Spill the Tea to the cactus that put you in my arms on the same day I found your porn collection—"

She laughed, her eyes flooding with tears that fell down her cheeks at a rapid rate.

"And then our visit to the tattoo shop that started your new addiction, our first kiss downtown while the flames of our love burned all around us."

She rolled her eyes, still laughing and crying, and I knew my speech was crap, but I wasn't done.

"You are my best friend, the love of my life, and my soul mate for eternity. Will you put me out of my misery and spend your life with me? Marry me, Chelsea Banks."

She was nodding viciously before I even finished my sentence, then she threw herself into my arms, her tears blending with mine as she kissed me.

"Yes, Liam." Her words were choked when she finally said them. "Of course I'll marry you. I love you so much."

I kissed her again, my heart feeling like it was about to burst in my chest. "I promise to always try to make you happy."

"You don't have to try." She shook her head and leaned it against mine. "We fit for a reason, Liam. Because we're better together just being ourselves, and I'll love you forever." She looked back at the shelf and shook her head with a laugh. "This is incredible." Then she turned back to me. "I just have one question."

"What is it, love?"

She tilted her head. "Why did you choose my second book and not my first?"

I grinned. "You can't guess?"

"Because it was inspired by our love story?" she asked.

"That's right, love. And—" I waggled my brows. "Willy and Sally's story may have ended, but ours will last forever."

Want to keep up with all the new releases in Vi Keeland and Penelope Ward's Cocky Hero Club world? Make sure you sign up for the official Cocky Hero Club newsletter for all the latest on upcoming books:

http://www.subscribepage.com/CockyHeroClub

Check out other books in the Cocky Hero Club series:
http://www.cockyheroclub.com

Thank you so much for reading *British Bachelor*. If you're a fan of steamy romance stories with unexpected depth just like this one, then you will love my *A Stolen Melody Duet*. Keep reading for an excerpt from book one, *Dangerous Hearts*, or grab it HERE free with Kindle Unlimited.

LET'S CONNECT!

I hope you enjoyed Chelsea and Liam's story! If you'd like to help spread the word about *British Bachelor*, reviews are the best way to let other readers know how you felt about a story. You can also connect with me on social media and sign up for my mail list. Be sure to never miss a new release, event, or sale!

Subscribe for Updates: www.smarturl.it/KK_MailList
K.K.'s Website & Blog: www.KKAllen.com
Facebook: www.Facebook.com/AuthorKKAllen
Goodreads: www.goodreads.com/KKAllen
BookBub: www.bookbub.com/profile/k-k-allen
Instagram: www.Instagram.com/KKAllen_Author

ACKNOWLEDGMENTS

Sometimes there are stories that are so much fun they pour out of me effortlessly. *British Bachelor* was that book for me this year. If you follow me on social media, then you'll know, I'm a die-hard Bachelor franchise fan. *The Bachelor*, combined with my deep love for Penelope Ward and Vi Keeland's story, *British Bedmate*, played a huge role in the inspiration that went in to bringing Liam and Chelsea's story to life.

Thank you, Penelope and Vi, for giving me this opportunity to write in your Cocky Hero Club world. I'm honored to be part of this series, and I will continue to be a huge fan of your stories.

Harloe Rae! My boo. I had a ridiculous amount of fun writing in tandem with you every single day. I can't wait for the romance world to get their hands on *Left for Wild*. You are pure magic and I love you.

I think my Alpha team #BossBabes almost had more fun reading than I did writing this story, haha. I couldn't have done it without you babes. Sammie, Cyndi, Richard, and

Renee. Adore you all so much. And a special shout out to my handsome British gent, Richard, who read over *British Bachelor* TWICE to make sure Liam was as authentic as possible. You are the best.

Once again, my #BetaBabes came in and ensured that I didn't muck anything up for Chelsea and Liam's story. Thank you so much Brenna, Patricia, Christine, and Kelly. Your highlights, honest critiques, and encouraging words were everything!

Thank you to my editors and proofreaders at Red Adept. I can always count on your team to bring me thorough edits to help strengthen my stories. Special thanks to Lynn, Taylor, and Amanda for all of your hard work and sweet words.

To my assistant, aka: my boss, Lindsey, who is always reading my mind and sending me a million and one reminders, always with a sweet and friendly demeanor. I love you forever.

To my Facebook street team, Angsters, my Instagram team, Booksters, and to my reader group, Forever Young. I love you babes with all my heart. Thank you for hanging with me and giving me some of my favorite places to hang on the interwebs.

To my book cover designer, Talia, at BookCoverKingdom! You are a dream to work with, thank you so much for giving me the best cover possible for this book.

To Christopher John at CJC Photography! We've been friends for nearly four years now and I'm so happy to finally get to work with you. Thanks for finding me a dreamy real-life Brit to be my Liam.

As always, to every reader and blogger who picks up this story (and made it this far), I couldn't do this without you. Thank you!

Much Love and HEAs,
K.K. Allen

BOOKS BY K.K. ALLEN

Sweet & Inspirational Contemporary Romance

Up in the Treehouse

Under the Bleachers

Through the Lens

Sweet and Sexy Contemporary Romance

Center of Gravity

Falling from Gravity

Defying Gravity

The Trouble with Gravity

Super Steamy Contemporary Romance

Dangerous Hearts

Destined Hearts

British Bachelor

Romantic Suspense

Waterfall Effect

A Bridge Between Us

Young Adult Fantasy

The Enchanted

The Equinox

The Descendants

Short Stories and Anthologies

Soaring

Echoes of Winter

Begin Again

Spring Fling

MORE INFO AT WWW.KKALLEN.COM

ABOUT THE AUTHOR

K.K. Allen is a *USA Today* bestselling and Romantic Times award-winning author who writes heartfelt and inspirational contemporary romance stories. K.K. is a native Hawaiian who graduated from the University of Washington with an Interdisciplinary Arts and Sciences degree and currently resides in central Florida with her ridiculously handsome little dude who owns her heart.

K.K.'s publishing journey began in June 2014 with a young adult contemporary fantasy trilogy. In 2016, she published her first contemporary romance, *Up in the Treehouse*, which went on to win the Romantic Times 2016 Reviewers' Choice Award for Best New Adult Book of the Year.

With K.K.'s love for inspirational and coming of age stories involving heartfelt narratives and honest emotions, you can be assured to always be surprised by what K.K. releases next.

www.KKAllen.com

Printed in Great Britain
by Amazon

20513411R00155